Have you got all the *Chestnut Hill* books?

Lauren Brooke

Chestnut Hill

Racing Hearts

■SCHOLASTIC

With special thanks to Elisabeth Faith

First published in the UK in 2009 by Scholastic Children's Books
An imprint of Scholastic Ltd
Euston House, 24 Eversholt Street
London, NW1 1DB, UK
Registered office: Westfield Road, Southam, Warwickshire, CV47 0RA
SCHOLASTIC and associated logos are trademarks
and or registered trademarks of Scholastic Inc

Series created by Working Partners

This edition published by Scholastic Ltd, 2013

Text copyright © Working Partners, 2009

Cover photography © Equiscot Photography

The right of Lauren Brooke to be identified as the
author of this work has been asserted by her.

ISBN 978 1407 13659 2

A CIP catalogue record for this book is available
from the British Library

Printed and bound by CPI Group (UK) Ltd, Croydon, CR0 4YY
Papers used by Scholastic Children's Books are made from
wood grown in sustainable forests.

1 3 5 7 9 10 8 6 4 2

www.scholastic.co.uk/zone

"You have to take the plunge sooner or later, Malory!" Carl O'Neil laughed as he unlocked the car trunk. "Might as well make it sooner."

Malory opened her door the tiniest fraction and let a waft of wintry air into the car. "It's gotta be minus ten out there!" she gasped. But already the warmth from the car heater was beginning to wear off and she realized she might as well vacate the vehicle. She eased herself out, tucking her scarf into the neck of her sweater.

"Plenty of activity, that's what you need," Mr O'Neil advised, his brown eyes twinkling. He piled her boot bag, riding hat and holdall into her arms. "You can start by carrying these in!"

"That's really generous of you, Dad," Malory puffed, pretending to buckle under the weight of her luggage. "But I'm more concerned about you. Old people are at greater risk of hypothermia in the winter, so I guess you should bring everything else!" Laughing at his look of mock outrage, she turned towards Adams

House. The dorm looked picture-postcard pretty in the frost, and warm yellow lights glowed in the downstairs windows. Malory adjusted the bulky holdall under her arm and walked carefully up the short flight of steps, wary of ice.

Once inside the foyer, she paused to adjust to the silence. Usually on the first day back to Chestnut Hill after a vacation there would hardly be room to stand among the crowds of students and parents. *It looks like I'm the first to arrive*, Malory thought. Her dad had needed to drop her off early so he could get back to open his shoe store. His manager had been visiting family in New York for the holidays, leaving Mr O'Neil single-handed.

A blast of cold air came into the foyer as Carl O'Neil walked in and put two cases down on the newly waxed floorboards. "I don't think I've ever known it this quiet." He dropped his voice to a stage whisper and looked exaggeratedly around the foyer. "Do you think we've come back on the wrong day?"

Malory grinned. "Just the wrong hour." She wouldn't want it to be the wrong day. As much as she'd loved Christmas with her dad, she couldn't wait to see her friends. She'd missed Lani, Dylan and Honey like crazy over the last three weeks.

"I thought I heard voices!" Mrs Herson, the housemistress, walked out of her apartment door on the far side of the hall. She was carrying a huge cut glass vase full of white chrysanthemums and red berries. Placing it on the table under the chandelier, she glanced across the polished mahogany surface with a warm smile of welcome. "Did you have a good vacation?"

"Great, thanks," Malory enthused. "Dad and I cooked up a huge Christmas dinner."

"I'll be eating leftovers for another week yet," Mr O'Neil joked as he patted his stomach. "I tried telling Mal it was just the two of us but she prepped enough veg for ten!" His eyes danced. "I hope you took advantage of the vacation to have a good rest, Mrs Herson. As for me, I'm about ready to go back to cosy evenings in front of the TV without having to argue over the remote control."

"Dad!" Malory protested. "Admit it, you're counting the days down until the mid-term break."

"I'll need that long to recover from carrying all of your luggage," Mr O'Neil groaned as he picked up her cases again.

"If you need anything just buzz my door," Mrs Herson told Malory. "It's good to have you back."

"It's good to be back," Malory replied. *Strike that*, she thought as she followed her dad to the curving double staircase that led up to the bedrooms. *It's absolutely brilliant to be back!*

Malory opened the door to the room she shared with Alexandra Cooper. Pale light fell from the windows on to the maple furnishings and twin beds. The room had the same quiet quality as the rest of the building and Malory's fingers itched to make up her bed with its cheerful checked duvet cover, and to spread out books and papers over her desk.

"Maybe I should take a picture." Mr O'Neil placed Malory's cases at the foot of the bed. "The start and end of term are the only times your room ever looks this tidy."

Impulsively Malory threw her arms around him. "I'm going to miss you so much!" The sweater she had given him for Christmas softly scratched against her cheek. "I don't expect you to wear this out in public, you know," she said pulling back to gaze at the top. The grey and lime diamond pattern hadn't seemed quite so loud when she'd purchased it.

"Are you kidding? It's the classiest piece in my wardrobe!" Mr O'Neil struck a pose in the full length mirror opposite Malory's bed. "I'm thinking of buying one for my manager and making it the official uniform for the store."

Malory laughed as she joined him in front of the mirror. She touched her new necklace made of aquamarine and diamanté, with an M-shaped pendant dangling from the centre. "I wish I could wear this as part of our official uniform," she said wistfully. Chestnut Hill had a strict code of what students could wear, and only a wristwatch and a pair of stud earrings were allowed when the girls were wearing the royal blue and grey uniform. The necklace from her father was by far her favourite present and she was touched by the thought her father had put into choosing it.

Mr O'Neil glanced at his watch. "I'm going to have to cut and run," he said reluctantly.

"I'll walk you down to the foyer." Malory's spirits took a nosedive.

As they walked down the corridor she tried to recall her earlier excitement about seeing her friends and beginning another new term, but it was hard to feel anything other than sadness at saying goodbye. They descended the carpeted stairs in silence and at the bottom her father turned to face her.

"Hey," he said, rubbing his finger under her chin as if she was a little girl again. "Don't look so sad."

"I'm sorry," Malory said. "I just hate saying goodbye."

"Then let's not say it," Mr O'Neil said, giving her a swift hug. His dark curly hair smelt faintly smoky from their living room's woodburner. "Let's say, see you soon."

Malory smiled. "That sounds much nicer."

"As soon as I get any spare time I'll drive out," Mr O'Neil promised as they headed to the front door. "Although you'll probably find it a tough call trying to squeeze me in around shopping at Cheney Falls, riding practice, swimming, party planning, black tie balls. . ."

"I'll never be too busy for you," Malory promised, giving him another hug.

"Ditto." He smiled before opening the door. A chill blast of air rushed in but Malory ignored it as she watched her father make his way down to the turning circle beyond the steps.

She responded to the cheery toot of the car's horn with an equally cheerful wave but inside she was missing her father already. *At least I'll be with my friends between now and mid-term. Dad will be spending every night in an empty flat.* She sighed. *If only Mom was still alive. . .* The wish was as futile now as every time before. Closing the door, she retraced her steps back to her room. The arrival of her friends suddenly felt a long way away.

Malory heaved her cases on to her bed and began transferring jumpers, jeans and T-shirts into her chest of drawers. Her riding clothes were hung carefully in the wardrobe, and she felt a rush of pride as she hooked the junior team T-shirt on to a hanger. Knowing she was captain of the junior jumping team still filled her with a mixture of awe and delight. *But this term I'm going to get a grip on the fact that I earned the title.* There was no way she was going to allow self-doubt to creep in as it had done before, helped in no small measure by fellow teammate Lynsey Harrison. *Lynsey might have a top show pony and have more A-Level circuit experience but that doesn't make her the best candidate for captain.* After a troubled term, Ali Carmichael, Director of Riding, had finally pointed out that she was looking for key personal qualities in the team's captain as well as riding ability, and that was why she had chosen Malory over Lynsey.

Closing the wardrobe door, Malory turned back to her case to take out the framed photo of Tybalt, Dylan's Christmas gift to her. She gazed down at the shot of the beautiful dark brown Thoroughbred staring over the paddock fence with his small neat ears pricked and his nostrils flared. The temperamental gelding was Malory's favourite horse on the yard, and since she was one of the few riders he would respond to, she had almost exclusive use of him.

As she was setting the photo down on her bedside table, there was a gentle rap on the door. Expecting Mrs Herson to walk in, Malory felt a jolt of surprised delight when a set of sparkling green eyes met her own. "Dylan!" she cried as the redhead stepped into the room. "What are you doing here?"

"Well, I did think of giving the first week of term a miss," Dylan Walsh replied. "After all, with my genius I could justify taking the time out. But I figured I might as well come back. I didn't want to leave you guys without the benefit of my wisdom."

"No kidding, Walsh." Lani Hernandez spoke dryly behind her. "Maybe you could remove your ego from the doorway? It's blocking my way."

Lani, too! Malory hurried to hug her friends before noticing a petite blonde-haired girl setting down two large cases in the corridor behind them. "Honey!"

"Dylan emailed us and suggested we all got here early so you wouldn't have hours hanging around on your own," Honey Harper said, throwing her arms around Malory.

"It's so great to see you all!" Malory exclaimed, touched by Dylan's thoughtfulness. "Although I wasn't sure you'd make it back with all the snow in Colorado" she added to Lani.

"I had my skis all waxed and was ready for an awesome run to the airport but there was a break in the weather and my dad was able to drive." Lani sounded regretful.

Dylan gave a shout of laughter. "I'd have given good

money to see that. I take it you were planning on balancing your luggage on your head!"

"Multi-talented, that's me." Lani grinned.

"How was Aspen?" Malory asked Dylan as they bundled into her room and sat cross-legged on her bed.

"Great, thanks," Dylan enthused. "I managed to do a black diamond run before leaving." She gave a dramatic sigh. "It was just a shame that I didn't have Henri there to admire my moment of greatness." The French boy she had crushed out on the previous year had this time holidayed at home. "Talking of cute boys, did you get to spend much time with Caleb?"

Malory felt her cheeks go pink at the mention of her boyfriend. "We got together before Christmas Day to swap presents," she answered, "and I met him here for the exhibition."

"Oh, the horsemanship clinic," Honey said. "I was going to come over to see that but we had family staying so I couldn't get away."

"So what did Caleb give you?" Dylan's eyes were bright with curiosity.

A little self-consciously, Malory held out her wrist to show them the delicate silver bracelet. "And he gave me a model horse carved out of amber," she added.

Honey lowered her head to examine the bracelet. "Oh, that's absolutely beautiful!" she gasped, her English accent notably more pronounced after two weeks with her family.

"So, what did you guys get?" Malory asked in an attempt to take the spotlight off her and Caleb.

"If we're talking from boyfriends then it's zero, zip, zilch." Dylan rolled her eyes in mock protest at her single status. "But my parents gave me a flying lesson which was cool. I got to go up in a light aircraft for two hours and had a go at controlling the plane myself."

Lani leaned over and placed her hands on Dylan's shoulders before looking into her eyes. "Promise me that if you ever take to the skies again and you're the one in the pilot's seat, you'll give me advance warning to seek out shelter."

"The instructor said I had real promise!" Dylan sounded injured.

"Real promise to wreak carnage?" The corners of Lani's mouth tugged up in a smile.

"Talking of real promise, what's new with you and Sam?" Dylan neatly turned the tables on Lani. "The last time we were messaging each other online you broke off to take a call from him."

"There was actually a break between phone calls this vacation?" Honey said teasingly. "It felt like the line was constantly engaged at our house." Her twin brother, Sam, had struck up a tentative romance with Lani last term.

Lani shrugged. "I'm a sucker for a hard luck story and Sam needs major help getting the lowdown on American football and baseball if he's going to click with the in crowd at St Kit's."

"Don't tell me, you're going to make him so with it, everyone's going to think he's never been without it," Malory chuckled. Sam had been in recovery from leukemia for the last two years, and was only just well enough to start attending the local boys' school.

"Just call me his personal cool guru." Lani gave a lazy smile.

"So I guess you didn't spend a whole load of time talking to Josh?" Malory asked Honey.

Honey's cheekbones tinged with colour. "We spoke a couple of times," she admitted.

"A day," Dylan added mischievously.

Honey jumped up. "Now we're all caught up, how about we go say hello to the first loves in our lives?"

"Good call." Malory unhooked her jacket from the back of the door. Since she lived close to the school, she was able to ride Tybalt during the holidays. But she always felt an extra rush of excitement to see him at the start of each new term. They had an important All Schools League competition to prepare for over the next few weeks, and she was determined that she and Tybalt were going to turn in their best performance yet!

As they headed down the stairs, Malory was surprised to hear voices floating up from the foyer. Had someone else turned up? Peering over the handrail she saw Patience Duvall and Lynsey Harrison standing at the door surrounded by cases. They waved their parents away before turning to hug each other.

"I guess we're not the only ones to arrive early," Malory commented.

Dylan gave a dramatic sigh. "There goes my few

hours' reprieve. I'd been planning on unpacking without receiving warnings from the fashion police."

Malory shot her friend a sideways glance and noticed Dylan's eyes were dancing with humour. *Although I'm not sure how long she'll stay upbeat about being Lynsey's roomie.* It had been a struggle last term, and Malory still wondered if Mrs Herson had been feeling mischievous when she paired Dylan with the one girl at Chestnut Hill that she really didn't get on with.

When she reached the foyer, Malory's gaze was drawn to Patience, who looked as if she had just got back from a summer vacation. Her olive complexion had deepened into a honey tan complementing her sun-streaked brown hair.

"You look amazing," Lynsey gushed, echoing Malory's thoughts. "Your whole ensemble is très chic."

"It's the French side of the family coming out," Patience explained, giving a twirl to show off her knee-length pinafore dress. She was wearing a cream woollen beret and matching gloves along with a swing coat which flared out as she moved.

"If she's not careful her legs will turn to popsicles," Dylan pointed out in a stage whisper. "The bare look is definitely not good in minus temperatures."

"So, how was Hawaii?" Lynsey asked, ignoring Dylan.

"Amazing." Patience stressed each syllable. "The ceremony was out of this world. Here. . ." She pulled a rolled up magazine out of a side pocket of her travel bag. "It made the centre page spread in *Society in Style*."

"Oh my gosh!" Lynsey exclaimed as she opened the magazine. "Talk about A-lister luck out! You could have filled an entire autograph book in the one day!"

Malory swapped a curious look with Honey. *What did Patience get up to this vacation?* she wondered.

Patience glanced up and held out the magazine. "Here," she offered, "take a look. I've got plenty more copies with me."

Dylan raised an eyebrow. "Um, why exactly would we want to do that?"

"Maybe it would help you figure a way to finally get some style savvy," Lynsey said sweetly as she shook back her long blonde hair.

Patience giggled. "It's a fashion magazine, not a magic wand."

"Oh, I'm sooo disappointed." Dylan's voice was heavy with sarcasm. "I just felt the opportunity to be turned into a devotee instead of an individual pass me by."

"The only thing these celebs are devoted to is trend-setting," Lynsey retorted. She jabbed her finger at the magazine in Malory's hands. "Look and learn."

Malory glanced down and read the title above the main photo: *Writer Edward Hunter Duval and his wife Marie-Claire, former French supermodel, renew their wedding vows at an intimate ceremony on the white sand beaches of Hawaii.*

"Your mother looks stunning!" Honey exclaimed as she peered at the magazine. Malory had to agree as she looked at the photos of the beautiful brunette in a strapless ivory gown, her hair tumbling down over her bare shoulders.

"Thanks." Patience smiled briefly. "Her Christmas present for me was a makeover and photo shoot in the morning. She wanted me to have the same full-on treatment that she had. She's *so* thoughtful. I've arranged for one of the posters of me to be framed and couriered over here. I'm going to hang it over my bed," she told Lynsey.

"I would have thought that the reflection in a mirror would be enough self-image in a room for any one person," Lani muttered.

"Ignore them," Lynsey instructed Patience. "They wouldn't know class if it jumped up and bit them on the nose."

"Or leaped out of a wardrobe dressed from head to toe in Dolce and Gabbana," Dylan parried.

"Hey, nice image, Walsh. You're a class act all on your own." Lani gave Dylan a high five.

Wearing matching pained expressions, Lynsey and Patience carried their cases over to the stairs.

"Do you think Patience's parents' wedding wasn't glitzy enough the first time around, so they had to have a repeat performance?" Dylan tucked her scarf into her coat as they stepped outside.

"I think it's sweet that they decided to renew their vows." Honey's breath sent a stream of vapour into the air. "I love looking through my parents' wedding album. They got married in this eighteenth-century parish church and my mum arrived in a horse-drawn carriage. I'd love it if they did it all over so Sam and I could be a part of it."

As they walked cautiously down the gritted path, Malory thought of her own parents' ceremony. They hadn't had an official photographer but the Polaroids taken by her grandparents had still managed to capture the love between her mum and dad as they made their vows under a flower-covered trellis. It had been the simplest of ceremonies in her grandparents' garden, with Malory's mum and dad going barefoot and wearing loose cotton outfits that they'd made themselves. *But that would have made it all the more special.* Malory felt a familiar ache at the hole left by her mother's death.

Dylan slipped her arm through Malory's. "I hope the weather warms up soon, otherwise I'll have to dig out Morello's snowshoes."

Malory glanced at her friend, grateful for the change of subject. She felt a gurgle of laughter at the thought of Morello attempting a course of jumps with glorified tennis racquets attached to his hooves. "I think it's set to get warmer mid-week."

Up ahead, Kelly, one of the stablehands, pushed a laden wheelbarrow towards the muck heap. "Hey guys, it's so great you're back! We've been keeping the horses in day and night while the ground is so hard, and we could really do with some help with all the extra mucking out."

"You mean, it's not our company that you're glad to have?" Honey called back.

"Sure it is!" Kelly winked. "Company with a shovel in one hand and a barrow in the other!"

"Whatever we end up doing, it's great to be back,"

Malory insisted, gazing around at the familiar stable yard. Already several horses had popped their heads over their doors to say hello. "There's no better place to kick start the New Year!"

2

Malory reached into her pocket and pulled out a horse cookie. "It's in my hand," she teased when Tybalt nuzzled hopefully at her jacket. The gelding lipped up the treat and Malory stroked his long dark-brown nose.

"Have you missed me?" she murmured. She hadn't been to see him in the last five days although it felt longer. *It's always hard being away. Vacations would be perfect if I could take Tyb home with me.* "But it's not like you could make the stairs up to the flat," she pointed out as she ducked down to refasten the surcingle that had come loose on Tybalt's stable rug. Straightening up, she slipped her arm over Tybalt's neck and gave him a hug. He smelled warm and comforting. Tybalt swung his head around in hope of another treat.

"No more, or you'll get spoilt," Malory scolded him. She brushed the back of her hand down his cheek. Tybalt's coat felt like velvet and as he gazed at Malory through his large dark eyes, her determination melted away. "Just one more," she relented, fishing out another cookie.

Noticing that Tybalt's tail was slightly matted and had some straw hanging in it, Malory decided to go to the tack room to fetch a water brush and comb. As she headed past Morello's stall she heard Dylan scolding the skewbald gelding: "You're not going to convince me that you need to put on an extra layer of blubber to keep out the cold!"

Looking over the half wall, Malory saw Dylan stuffing hay through the grill that divided Morello's stall from the one next door. "What are you doing?"

Dylan glanced over her shoulder. "Can you believe Morello's sweet-talked Skylark into passing her hay through to him?" She brushed her hands off against her jeans and walked over to the door. Behind her, Morello gave a soft whicker. A moment later Skylark appeared on the other side of the grill and proceeded to push a mouthful of hay through a gap in the bars.

Dylan rolled her eyes as Malory giggled. "I'm going to go talk to Sky instead and see if I can point out to her that Morello's not starving."

Malory left her to it and carried on down the aisle. As she drew closer to the tack room, Lynsey's voice rang out. "Look at Blue's water bucket! It's got mud all over it. If the outside's dirty, then the inside's probably the same. This is what happens when I leave him here over the vacation. I won't be doing it again!"

Patience was standing outside the stall belonging to Lynsey's top show pony, Bluegrass. "You're going to have to complain," she told her friend. "You're entitled to expect the best of care for Blue."

Malory would have loved to duck past and let the situation simmer down but, knowing it would be good for team morale if bridges were built between her and Lynsey, she walked over to the stall. "Blue looks happy to see you," she said, looking over the half wall. The roan's eyes were fixed adoringly on Lynsey. Lynsey's expression softened as she turned to rub Bluegrass' nose. "It's great to see him, too," she admitted. "Although I didn't think I'd end up regretting leaving him over the vacation."

"He looks in top shape to me," Malory observed as she looked at Bluegrass' clear eyes, shining coat and pricked ears.

"I'm totally tuned into Blue and I always know when he's not a hundred per cent on form." Lynsey was insistent as she unbuckled the chest straps on the roan's rug.

"I guess any difference in him could be down to missing you," Malory suggested. She knew the standards of horse care at Chestnut Hill were excellent, and there was no way Bluegrass would have suffered from staying there over Christmas.

Lynsey waved her hand dismissively. "It's more likely because he's not getting the right care without me here to keep an eye on things. Blue isn't used to having a single glitch in his stable management. With his breeding, the slightest change can make him off colour. He's not an *average* pony."

Which was what, Malory acknowledged with a wince, Lynsey considered most of the other ponies on the yard to be, even though many of them had excellent show pedigrees. Biting back the comment that all of the horses on the yard received top care, Malory tried to look sympathetic. She was determined that there would be some new unity in the junior team this term. "I'm sure Bluegrass has been really well looked after, but now you're here you can make sure he gets everything he's used to."

Before Lynsey could respond a cheerful voice sounded from behind. "Is everything OK?"

Turning around Malory saw Ali Carmichael, the riding director, and also Dylan's aunt. Strands of brown hair had escaped from her ponytail and hung in soft tendrils around her face, and her cheeks were pink from being out in the cold.

"Bluegrass' bucket is dirty." Lynsey got straight to the point.

"I'll get it replaced with a clean one," Ali Carmichael said pleasantly. She turned to Malory, her blue eyes warm. "Have you been to see Tybalt yet? He's spent the last few days hanging over his stable door pricking his ears at every sound and then looking disappointed when it didn't turn out to be you."

Maory felt a rush of delight at the thought that Tybalt had missed her, maybe as much as she had missed him. "I've just been to say hi."

Ms Carmichael was holding a laminated sheet of A4. "I'm about to pin this up on the noticeboard. It's a copy of this term's module, Show Equitation. It'll be particularly interesting to those of you on the team, who might like to try some other types of competition this year." She walked away, humming a Christmas carol.

Malory bit her lip. She knew that to score well in competitions judged on equitation, horses needed to turn in a flawlessly stylish performance and while there was no doubting Tybalt's beauty and grace, flawless was something they were still working on.

"Another term where Bluegrass isn't going to be stretched," Lynsey commented as she opened the door to the stall. "His equitation is perfect." She shot Malory a sideways glance. "Although that can't be said for the rest of the junior team."

"Then I guess it's a good thing we're practising it this term," Malory said levelly, determined not to rise to the bait. If being team captain meant exercising patience then that's exactly what she would do. Although she wouldn't be at all surprised if over the next few weeks Lynsey pushed it to the outer limits!

Malory sank down on one of the sofas in the Adams common room, grateful for the soft cushions beneath her. She was surprised at how tired she felt. "Whoever thought up Saturday being the first day of a new term should be given a prize," she yawned. "It's so great to think that it's Sunday and not Monday tomorrow."

Lani looked up from the book she was reading in the opposite chair. "Agreed. If anyone dares wake me up before ten tomorrow I'll put a hex on them."

"You're taking up witchcraft now?" Honey put down a tray of hot chocolates she had made in the kitchenette.

"If it's good enough for Hermione Granger. . ." Lani

grinned before shaking her head. "It's all a load of hocus pocus, if you ask me. But at least you all now get my point that I want my beauty sleep tonight."

"Hey guys, have you seen this?" Dylan sat down alongside Malory and handed her a postcard. On the front was a group of costumed dancers wearing lederhosen and frilled white shirts, and underneath was emblazoned, *Bavaria*. "Matilda Harvey sent us a card," Dylan said as Malory turned it over and began reading the small, neat writing aloud.

"*To all my friends in Adams House, hello from Bavaria, and a very happy New Year! I'm spending my vacation here and have had a great time seeing all the amazing sights. I bought a hand-carved cuckoo clock from a market stall today and it reminded me of you all and what a talented bunch you are!*"

"She's going easy on us. We might have had a masterclass in decoration-making from her, but producing hand-carved cuckoo clocks? I don't think so!" Dylan interrupted.

Malory laughed before continuing. "*I've still got another five days left to go here although I suspect they'll fly by. I hope you all had a great vacation and once you're back at Chestnut Hill you'll still find time to get crafty!*" The bottom of the card was signed with an artistic flourish, *Matilda Harvey*. Malory got up and passed the card to Razina Jackson who was playing chess with Alexandra. "It's a postcard from Matilda. Remember, she came at the end of last term to give us some tips on making Christmas decorations?"

"Sweet," Razina said, taking the card from her.

Alexandra left her chair to look more closely at the card. "It's really kind of her to write us," she commented.

"Yeah, she's really thoughtful," Malory agreed as she turned back to the sofa and settled back against the squishy cushions. "With her store being across the street from Dad's, she sometimes takes around a meal she's cooked the night before."

Dylan raised her eyebrows. "She must cook a lot to be able to feed her own family plus your dad."

"She lives on her own." Malory picked up her mug and breathed in the chocolatey aroma before taking a sip.

Dylan's eyes brightened. "So if she's lonely I guess she must like spending time with your dad?"

Malory frowned. "I don't think they spend time together, exactly. She just pops in every now and then with something to eat. And she doesn't come across as lonely. She always seems busy when I see her."

"But your dad keeps busy and you worry about him being lonely so why should it be any different for Matilda?" Dylan pushed.

"Why are you so keen for her to be lonely, Dyl?" Lani asked.

"I don't want her to be lonely," Dylan said impatiently. "I'm just saying that it would be helpful if she was."

Lani frowned. "You're going to have to explain to me how that's different."

Malory got the feeling she knew where Dylan was

going, in her usual runaway locomotive style. "You're not thinking of turning your matchmaking skills on my dad, are you?"

Dylan grinned. "My work is done with getting you guys fixed up. So until you're all ready to hire me as your wedding planner I might as well kill time working my magic on some other singletons. The only person it never seems to work for is me!"

Malory felt a stab of alarm. "I'm not so sure my dad wants a wand waved over him."

"But it wouldn't do any harm to see if he might like to date Matilda," Honey pointed out.

"Only if you could handle it, though." Lani sounded concerned as she looked at Malory. "Your dad hasn't seen anyone since your mom died, has he?"

Lani was being a little blunt, but she had a good point. *Could I handle it?* Malory wondered. Matilda was really nice and there was no doubting she'd be great company for her dad. She was pretty, smart and funny. *It's selfish of me to want to keep Dad just to myself, especially since I'm away at school so much.* Taking a deep breath, she looked at her friends. "I could handle it. I think."

"Game on!" Dylan exclaimed. She jumped up and headed over to retrieve the postcard from Razina. "Matilda's flying home today," she said after checking the date on the postcard, "so we can set up a date anytime soon."

"How about we book them a table for dinner next weekend?" Lani suggested.

Malory shook her head. This was all happening way

too fast. She didn't even know if her dad wanted to start dating again! "Let's keep it simple," she said. "A coffee will do."

"Yes, but just a coffee might not give Matilda the message that your dad wants to date her," Dylan pointed out.

"We don't know if he does." Malory was beginning to wonder if this was a good idea.

Dylan leaned forward with her hands on her knees, looking very earnest. "Mal, your dad probably *needs* our help to meet someone. It must be hard for him, living on his own, running the store, out of practice with the whole dating thing. . ."

Malory didn't want Dylan to portray her dad as quite so lonely and cut off from society. "He's not unhappy!" she protested.

Lani put her hand on Malory's arm. "Honestly, we're not saying that he is. But don't you think he'd like to spend more time with Matilda? He's such a sweet guy, maybe he hasn't plucked up courage to ask her out yet!"

Malory had to admit that could be right where her dad was concerned. Though she wasn't sure she had helped his dating chances much with her choice of patterned Christmas sweater.

"How about lunch?" Honey said practically. "It's enough to give them a chance to get together if they decided that's what they want but not as full on as a dinner date. There's a really nice Italian restaurant in Cheney Falls which does a special lunchtime deal.

My parents took Sam and me there one Saturday last term."

"OK." Malory decided to let her friends make their plans, knowing it was easier to let them have their own way. "Now all we have to do is work out how to get them both there."

"No problem." Honey smiled. "We can phone Matilda and ask if she can come shopping with us next Saturday to help choose supplies for our new craft club."

"What new craft club?" Dylan asked.

"I suddenly feel the urge to create one." Honey's blue eyes twinkled.

"Brilliant double whammy!" Lani leaned forward to give Honey a high five. "So Mal can ask her dad to meet her at the restaurant while we suggest to Matilda that we stop off there after finishing our shopping. Then all we have to do is leave the two of them to it!"

Malory nodded, trying to ignore the worm of anxiety that had uncurled in her stomach. Would her dad appreciate them getting involved in his private life? What about Matilda? She might even be dating someone already! There was so much that could go wrong. But looking at the delighted expressions on her friends' faces, Malory kept her concerns to herself. Instead she slipped her hand behind her back and crossed her fingers. *Please let this work out!*

"I think I'm suffering from the Monday blues," Dylan groaned as she put her tray down on the table.

"Well the fact that it's double riding after lunch

should chase them away," Honey said, sprinkling parmesan over her lasagne.

"Your problem is that you have no stamina, Walsh." Lani looked flushed with excitement as she joined them.

"No, my problem is I'm suffering from prep overload," Dylan retorted. "Madame Dubois has flipped, if you ask me. A pop quiz on French verbs on Wednesday and an essay on our vacation to hand in by Friday! Hasn't she heard of easing back in?"

"Easing, schmeasing," Lani said, plunging a fork into her spaghetti and twisting it neatly.

"OK," Dylan said, pushing away her club sandwich. "I want what she's got." She nodded theatrically at Lani. "It's like having a cheerleader sitting next to me!"

Lani grinned. "Dr Duffy has selected me and three others from the science club to design a new invention. The top two projects will get published in a national junior science magazine. I've had these great ideas for measuring baseball speeds and trajectories to maximise the flight of the ball."

"On the other hand. . ." Dylan pulled her plate back.

"I'm going to eat and then go over to the student centre and email Sam to see if he's got any ideas," Lani continued, as if Dylan hadn't spoken. "How about you come with me, Mal? You could email Matilda and your dad."

"That's a good idea." Honey nodded. "We need to give them plenty of warning so they don't make any other plans."

Malory swallowed, feeling her insides twist with nerves. "What if one of them can't make it?"

"No problem," Dylan told her. "Either we'll get all of the stock we need to set up our new craft club, or you'll have a fantastic catch-up lunch with your dad."

"It's a win-win situation," Honey added.

"I hope so," Malory said fervently. "I really hope so."

Malory replaced her grooming kit before lifting Tybalt's gleaming tack from its rack. She cradled the saddle on one arm and shoved the bridle on to her shoulder. *I wonder how long it will take before I get replies from Matilda and Dad?* she wondered. She'd thought about practically nothing else since sending out her invites.

"Watch out!" Jennifer Quinn called, ducking down to pick up the reins which were trailing on the ground.

"Thanks." Malory pulled a face. "I'm so not with it right now."

"You'd better get with it once you're on Tybalt, or it won't be just the reins on the ground," Jennifer teased.

Fair point, Malory acknowledged as she left the room and walked up the aisle. *Particularly since I haven't ridden Tybalt in just over a week.*

"Hey, Mal. Tybalt's raring to go. He's playing soccer with his stable door," Abigail Loach said as she hurried by with a grooming kit.

Tybalt tossed his head when he saw Malory, his dark eyes glowing with enthusiasm. "You look as if you've just eaten a bucket of coffee beans," Malory teased as she let herself into the stall. She wasn't unnerved by his high spirits; in fact, she liked the challenge of persuading him to co-operate when he just wanted to dance on the spot.

Across the aisle, one of the horses gave a high-pitched whinny. Tybalt gave a piercing response before spinning in a circle, churning up his straw bed.

"Like Abi said," Malory puffed, taking hold of Tybalt's headcollar. "Raring to go!"

After tacking the gelding up, she led him out to the yard and mounted. The moment she closed her legs against him, Tybalt stepped forward eagerly. Malory steered him over to the indoor barn and paused in the entrance while Lynsey trotted by on Bluegrass. "Let's go," Malory said, nudging Tybalt down the centre line once the other pair was safely inside. With just two of them in the arena they had plenty of space to work independently while waiting for the rest of the class to join them.

She worked Tybalt on a steadily decreasing circle to encourage him to drop his head, accept the bit, and work harder with his hindquarters. The moment he tried to avoid her hands by lifting his head and hollowing his back, she drove him forward in a working trot, half halted and then changed the rein.

"Good work!" Ali Carmichael called to Malory from the centre of the arena. "Keep him busy until he's worn off his surplus energy."

Before long the arena had filled and Malory joined on the end of the ride behind Morello, who had flattened his ears at Dylan's request for a working trot.

"It's me who's recovering from too much Christmas cake, not you!"

Dylan's exasperated voice floated back to Malory, who tried not to smile. Many of the school's ponies were used for riding lessons during the vacation and it often took them a few sessions to switch out of sluggish riding-school mode.

"Hi, everyone! I hope you all had a great vacation," Ali Carmichael called out. "Today's session is going to be all about getting you back into condition after a couple of weeks of overindulgence. I'm sure by now you've all received copies of the equitation module and, just to warn you, the All Schools League competition this term is holding equitation classes." She glanced around. "Your homework between now and our next session is to read up on exactly what equitation is!"

Malory's arms were beginning to ache from Tybalt pulling on the reins. She half halted him again to stop him crowding Morello and hoped that the gelding would soon settle.

"First of all I'd like you to quit your stirrups and trot around the arena, changing the rein at M," Ms Carmichael announced.

Malory transferred her reins into one hand before bending down to pick up each stirrup and crossing the leathers in front of the saddle. She sank her weight down through her heels, even though she no longer had stirrup irons supporting her feet, and concentrated on sitting deep in the saddle. After five minutes she felt cramping pains in her side. *I'm more out of condition than I thought!*

"OK, lengthen the distance between you and the horse in front so that you're all equally spaced around the arena," Ali Carmichael told them. She waited until the class was strung out. "Now everyone turn in to face me and halt."

Tybalt's halt was ragged and his reluctance to stand still was clear when he began to paw at the ground. Across the arena Lynsey rolled her eyes. Bluegrass was standing perfectly square, his neck arched and his hocks tucked neatly underneath him.

"Easy, Tyb," Malory whispered, stroking the Thoroughbred's neck.

"I know that some of you are going to regard today's session in terms of physical punishment instead of physical education," Ali Carmichael smiled, "but every exercise we do has a specific purpose to improve your position, confidence, posture, balance, suppleness and co-ordination. For anyone who's already done their homework on equitation you'll know this is all great groundwork! For today I'd like to start with your legs. Nearly straighten your left leg, then lift it away from the saddle and slightly back."

Malory almost let out a groan as her thigh muscles protested.

"OK, left legs back in position, and when you're ready, repeat with your right leg." Ali Carmichael walked towards Abigail and adjusted her leg for her. "This exercise opens your hips and helps you gain a deeper seat," she explained. "I know it feels uncomfortable right now but I promise you'll feel the benefits."

They worked through twenty minutes of exercises at halt and walk and when Ms Carmichael finally called an end to them Malory was aching all over. *But it's good aching, not bad*, she realized as she lined up in the centre of the arena.

"That was more brutal than any gym workout," Dylan groaned as she halted beside Malory. "I'm just glad Morello is in sluggish mode today. If he was feeling feisty and had decided to quit the arena, I wouldn't have the energy to stop him."

"Oh don't worry, Tybalt can provide enough fireworks all on his own," Lynsey said from further up the line.

Malory gazed ahead, pretending not to have heard Lynsey's jibe. Right on cue, Tybalt lowered his head and ran back two steps. When Malory squeezed him back on to the bit he gave an annoyed swish of his tail.

"You've all worked really hard," Ms Carmichael said. "And I'm sure you'll be pleased to know that I won't be giving over any more sessions to exercising."

Lani gave a small cheer.

Ali Carmichael smiled. "But I would suggest that you incorporate some of the exercises into your warm-up sessions from now on."

"I'll be trying to forget them, not practise them," Dylan whispered.

"We're going to finish up today with a small fixed fence." Ali Carmichael waved her hand at the tiger trap in the lower half of the arena. "Mal, why don't you take Tybalt over first?"

Malory trotted Tybalt away and circled him before pushing him into a canter. As they rode toward the triangular fence, Tybalt increased his speed. Malory tried to half halt him but Tybalt ignored her aids and pulled against her hands. The fence loomed up and Malory knew Tybalt was going too fast. He stood well back from the fence and launched into the air, forcing Malory to grab a handful of mane to keep her balance. On landing he gave two bucks before Malory was able to get him back on to the bit and under control.

"Don't worry, Tybalt's just full of beans today," Ali Carmichael called. "Or should that be full of oats?"

As Malory rode back to the line, she could feel Lynsey's gaze boring into her. *OK, it wasn't exactly our best performance but it's our first session back.* Leaning down, she patted Tybalt's damp neck. "We'll show them next time," she murmured.

So much for building morale on the jumping team! Tybalt seemed determined to prove that Lynsey was right when she said he was too unreliable to be the captain's ride.

3

Malory woke an hour before her alarm was set to go off on Saturday morning. Lying in bed, she stared at the pale morning light seeping around the edge of the curtain and debated trying to get back to sleep. But as she started to remember what was due to happen that day, she knew she didn't have a chance of dropping off again.

Both her father and Matilda had taken up her invitation to meet – though of course they only thought they were meeting her and her friends, not each other – and the plan to get them together was just hours away from being a success or a disaster. Sitting up, Malory tugged on a pair of socks before padding quietly into the en suite. She showered and took her time applying eye shadow and lip gloss. When she finally went back into their room Alexandra was up and dressed.

"I'm going down to the library to do some extra cramming," she told Malory as she zipped up her ankle boots.

"Oh, right, it's the general knowledge tournament this afternoon." It had clean gone out of Malory's mind. "Good luck. Not that you'll need it with your awesome memory!"

Alexandra gave a self-conscious smile. "We're up against some pretty stiff competition. Wycliffe College haven't been knocked off the top spot in the last three years."

"Time for a change then," Malory told her.

Alexandra stood up and shouldered her bag. "See you later."

"Later," Malory echoed. She unhooked the jeans and hoodie she'd hung on her wardrobe door the night before and slipped them on. After running a brush through her curly black hair, she had to admit she was ready. There was no more delaying. Taking a deep breath, she picked up her coat and purse and left for the student centre.

Honey was already at their favourite table on the far side of the canteen. Malory selected scrambled eggs on toast and freshly squeezed orange juice before going to join her.

"All set for Operation Lunchdate?" Honey greeted her.

"I feel as if it's the morning of a jumping competition," Malory confessed as she sat down. "Even my butterflies have butterflies!"

"It will be fine," Honey said reassuringly. "Matilda and your dad are both such nice people, they're sure to get along."

"I just hope they don't feel awkward and end up spending the entire time trying to think of something to say," Malory said, pushing some eggs on to a bit of toast.

"I'm more worried about whether Matilda will agree to go to the restaurant with us." Dylan joined them bearing a full cooked breakfast, a fruit salad and a croissant. "What if she helps us buy the craft stuff and then has to dash off?"

"Then I get a nice, stress-free meal with my dad," Malory said. When there was a pause, she glanced up at her friends' surprised faces. "Oops, did I say that out loud?"

"If you don't want to go through with it we don't have to," Honey said gently.

"Are you kidding?" Dylan exclaimed. "Of course Mal wants to go through with it. We're talking about her dad's happiness here."

"No, we're not." Malory was alarmed. "He's happy already. All we're talking about is setting him up with some company."

Lani set her tray down. "Hi, what have I missed?"

"Mal's having second thoughts about Operation Lunchdate." Honey pushed back her chair to go and get her glass refilled.

Malory shook her head. "Forget I said anything. I'm doing that glass half-empty instead of half-full thing and thinking of everything that could go wrong today instead of what could go right."

"Wow." Lani blinked as she sat down. "Probably best to stop thinking."

Malory watched Honey come back. Her friend was wearing lacy tights, biker boots and a tartan mini flared dress, topped with a tan leather jacket, fingerless gloves and a baker boy hat. "I love your new look," she said to Honey, aiming for a change of subject.

"Thanks. My gran sent the outfit over for my Christmas present," Honey told her as she sat back down.

"I wish my nan was cool enough to be into the London fashion scene," Dylan commented. "I got an encyclopaedia disc set."

Malory leaned her arms on the table. "Did your gran send the purse too?"

Honey unhooked the mauve suede purse off the side of her chair and passed it over. "My aunt sent this as a craft project. I've sewed on all the pieces but I think it needs some extra decorations. I'm going to look out for some ideas while we're shopping with Matilda."

"You've done a great job on the stitching." Malory admired the bag as she turned it over and ran her hand over the soft fabric.

"Hey, didn't I see one of those in *Society in Style*?" Lynsey's voice, laced with sarcasm, broke in on them.

Glancing up, Malory saw Lynsey and Patience heading to the adjoining table.

"Maybe," Dylan called after them. "But Honey wouldn't know as she doesn't follow fashion, she prefers to set it."

Lani grinned. "You got her there."

"It's just the start of everything going right today." Dylan looked at Malory. "And I mean *everything!*"

The wind whipped Malory's cheeks as she stepped off the minibus, and she hugged her coat closer. "Do you think it's going to snow?"

"If it does it will be just a few romantic flurries, nothing more," Dylan said confidently as she slipped her arm through Malory's.

They headed up the shop-lined street which was still strung with twinkling fairy lights from the holiday displays. Turning down a narrow side street, they approached *Verdi's*, the glass-fronted Italian restaurant that was the venue for Operation Lunchdate. The sign on the door showed CLOSED but as they drew nearer it was twisted around to OPEN.

"Perfect timing," Honey said with satisfaction in her voice.

Lani pushed open the door and they filed inside. Violin music was playing softly in the background, adding to the romantic atmosphere. The seating areas were sectioned off by vine-covered wrought iron panels, and the cushions were covered in soft pink and cream fabric. Bowls of candles flickered on each table, sending warm yellow light across the cream tablecloths.

"Ah, ladies, a table for four?" The maitre d' closed the door behind them.

Malory's mouth felt dry. "Um, for two, please. At half past one?"

"No problem." The maitre d' walked over to a walnut lectern to write down their booking. "And the name?"

"O'Neil," Malory told him. "Carl O'Neil."

"That table would be perfect," Dylan suggested, pointing to a table for two set in a wall alcove. "It's a romantic lunch date," she added, her eyes sparkling with enthusiasm.

The maitre d' smiled. "Ah, then no other table will do a better job. I shall make a note of it for you."

Malory felt her spirits rise as they walked back out into the street. It was a lovely restaurant and the perfect setting for her father and Matilda to get to know each other better.

"OK, guys." Dylan checked their schedule on her BlackBerry. "We're due to meet Matilda in five minutes. Mal, you're meeting your dad in fifteen outside Starbucks. That gives us an hour with Matilda to shop for our fictitious craft club before suggesting we go to *Verdi's* for lunch."

"Who said it has to be fictitious?" Honey protested. "I like the idea of starting up a craft club."

"I guess that makes you the president, then," Lani said.

"Great," Honey said happily. "That means I get final say on the materials we buy today."

Dylan grinned. "Admit it, Lani. She just won on a technicality!"

They made their way to the stone fountain outside the main entrance to the mall where they had arranged to meet Matilda. Malory spotted her coming towards them through the crowds, unmistakable in a scarlet beret and matching scarf over a mustard-coloured swing coat. She waved. "Matilda! Over here!"

Matilda dodged around a woman with a double pushchair and joined them, her cheeks and nose pink from the cold January air. Strands of dark red hair had escaped from the beret and curled around her face. She hugged Malory before turning to greet the other girls. "I was so excited when I got your email about wanting to start up a craft club! I'm really honoured that you'd like my input in getting it up and running."

Faced with Matilda's generous spirit, Malory couldn't help feeling a twinge of guilt at their deception.

"I don't think we're going to need a huge amount to begin with because there are only four members so far," Honey told her, "but maybe you could suggest some projects to get started on and tell us what we need to buy?"

Well done, Honey, Malory thought as Matilda's hazel eyes lit with enthusiasm.

"How about you start off making a calendar for the new year?" Matilda suggested. "I know that these days you all have electronic gadgets but there's nothing nicer than something visual hanging on a wall. And how about some handmade thank you cards for all of the gifts you got for Christmas? It sure beats emails!"

"That sounds terrific," Honey enthused.

"I know a great stall that will have all you need to kick-start your craft club," Matilda said, turning towards the precinct.

"Actually –" Dylan's eyes twinkled " – we thought we'd call it the Crafty Club."

Well, I guess we are being crafty. . . "I'd love to come but I've arranged to meet my dad," Malory put in, taking her cue. "I'll catch up with you guys later."

"Say hi to your dad for me," Matilda told her.

Malory flashed a smile before hurrying away. Matilda was so nice! Malory hoped she would forgive them for setting her up like this.

Starbucks was close to where the minibus had dropped them off. Carl O'Neil was already waiting outside with a thick blue scarf wrapped around his neck. His face lit up when he saw Malory and he held out his arms. She ran straight into them, breathing in the familiar scent of aftershave.

"This is a great honour, my daughter choosing lunch with her aged father over shopping with her friends," he teased.

"Hey, not so much of the old," Malory said, stepping back. Her father was actually in great shape, she realized, never having given the thought much attention before. His thick black hair had only a tiny smattering of grey at his temples and his face was unlined apart from the creases at the corners of his blue eyes when he smiled.

"Well, I certainly feel the cold more than I did when I was your age," he commented with a laugh. "How about we get a hot chocolate to warm up before we do anything else?"

"Sure," Malory said, thrilled to be with her dad again

but on tenterhooks that they would bump into Matilda and the others.

After their hot chocolate they visited the second-hand bookshop. As usual Malory scoured the shelves for anything on horses, and was thrilled when she found an autobiography of Pippa Funnell, a famous British eventer. Her dad selected two crime thriller paperbacks. "I need something to keep me company during the long winter nights now you're back at school," he joked as he took them over to the shop counter. "Now, how about lunch?"

Malory glanced at her watch. If they went now they'd be a little early. *Which is better than leaving it to the last minute and arriving at the door at the same time as the others,* she thought. "I've booked us a table," she told her father as they stepped back out on to the high street. "It's a small Italian restaurant that Honey recommended."

Carl O'Neil's eyebrows shot up. "I figured we'd be doing our usual burger and fries followed by a bucket of popcorn and a movie. What's the occasion?"

"They do a special lunchtime deal." Malory bit her lip. Had they made a mistake in booking a table at a fancy place? She knew money was tight for her father. In spite of her scholarship at Chestnut Hill there were still extra expenses to meet that put a drain on his pocket.

"It's not the cost I'm worried about," her father reassured her as they turned down the side street. "I assumed you'd prefer something a bit more, well, casual. I guess I sometimes forget how fast you're growing up."

"I haven't outgrown burger and fries." Malory smiled. "I just thought it would be nice to do something a bit different today." *Oh boy, are we doing something different!*

The maitre d' took their coats before leading Malory and her father over to the table set for two. He gave Malory a slightly puzzled smile as he handed her the menu. "Can I get you anything to drink?"

Remembering that they had booked the table for a romantic lunch, Malory desperately hoped the maitre d' wouldn't mention it. "I'm OK, thanks," she told him. "Maybe we could get a jug of water?"

"I think the O'Neil budget will stretch to a soda," her father murmured as the maitre d' walked away.

Malory felt herself turn red. She hoped she wouldn't have to carry on with the charade for much longer. "I'm still fine after the hot chocolate," she told him.

Before Mr O'Neil could respond the restaurant door opened and Dylan walked in with Matilda. Honey and Lani were just a step behind.

"Guys, look who's here!" Dylan exclaimed, waving at Malory and Mr O'Neil.

Malory pushed back her chair. "Hey, why don't we all eat together?" Her voice sounded unconvincing as she shot her father a nervous glance. Mr O'Neil raised his eyebrows and Malory could tell he'd guessed what was going on.

"That's a great idea." Lani picked up a menu from an empty table and glanced at it. "But I'm not sure I feel like Italian food today."

"Well, how about we go grab a burger?" Honey suggested.

Malory looked at Matilda. Her cheeks felt on fire, but she couldn't stop now. Dylan had told them all exactly what to say, as if they were actors putting on a play. "We wouldn't want to spoil your and Dad's meal," she blurted out. "You go ahead and eat here."

Matilda's eyes were wide with surprise as she glanced at Carl O'Neil.

Rising from his chair, Mr O'Neil apologized. "Please don't think you have to. . ."

"Are you kidding? I'm starving and Italian is just what I feel like. I hear they do an amazing Carbonara here." Matilda sat down in the chair Malory had just vacated and shrugged off her coat.

"I think our job here is done," Dylan murmured to Malory as Mr O'Neil sat back down.

"I'll see you later, Dad," Malory said. She wondered if she sounded as apologetic as she felt.

"Later," Mr O'Neil replied, his expression inscrutable.

"Are you going to eat that?" Dylan asked Malory.

Malory stared down at her burger and shook her head. She had completely lost her appetite. "You have it." She pushed her plate across the table.

"I'm sure they're getting on fine." Honey reached out to squeeze Malory's arm. "You saw how well Matilda took it."

"I'm more worried about the fact that I tricked my

dad," Malory said unhappily. "He knows that the whole thing was a set-up. I've never done anything like this before."

"Don't forget, they're friends already. It's not like you've set him up with a total stranger," Dylan tried to reassure her.

"He's going to know you did it for all the right reasons," Lani added before draining her milkshake. She glanced at her watch. "We've been away for an hour. Shall we give them more time?"

"Yes," Dylan said. She propped her chin on her hands and gazed dreamily out of the window. "They could be lost in conversation, finding out all this cool stuff they have in common, choosing a dessert to share, ordering coffee while the waiters clear up around them. . ."

"No." Malory was firm. "I want to go and see them now. If they've enjoyed themselves, they can arrange to see each other again."

"And if they haven't, at least we can end any awkwardness by turning up." Honey was siding with Malory. She slipped off her chrome stool and pushed her arms into her jacket. "Come on, guys. I'm dying to see how it went."

The restaurant was a five minute walk away. As they drew closer, Malory stopped and looked at her friends. "Do you mind if I go in on my own?" she asked. "It's just that it will be a bit crowded if we all walk up to the table." She also wanted to face her dad on her own, rather than hiding among everyone else. She'd changed her mind about Operation Lunchdate as soon as they'd met Matilda outside the mall, and she just hoped their meal hadn't been a complete disaster.

"No, that's fine. We'll wait out here," Honey said.

"Wish me luck," Malory said, her heart thumping uncomfortably.

"Good luck," her friends chorused.

She pushed open the door and headed through the half-full restaurant. Her dad and Matilda were facing each other over small white coffee cups. At least they'd made it to the end of the meal. . . Relief flooded Malory as they both burst into laughter over something Matilda had said. Had Operation Lunchdate been a success after all?

She hesitated between two tables, unsure if she should intrude, but just as she was thinking of backing away, Matilda caught her eye. "Hey, Malory!" She beckoned her over.

Malory walked up to the table. "Did you have a nice meal?"

"Lovely, thanks." Matilda's smile was warm. "But I have to run now if I'm going to catch my afternoon appointment." She looked across at Carl O'Neil. "Thank you so much for lunch. I don't think I've had so much fun since the last time we went out."

Mr O'Neil stood up to help Matilda with her coat. "It was great," he agreed. "I'll see you in the next day or so."

Dropping a kiss on Malory's cheek and enveloping her in a cloud of flowery perfume, Matilda left.

Malory stared at her dad in astonishment. "Does this

mean you've already been out on a date together?" she gasped as soon as Matilda was out of earshot.

"Not exactly," Mr O'Neil said as he zipped up his own coat. "Last week I went out with her and her boyfriend, Ashley, who works in Washington DC."

Malory's spirits plummeted. "Oh."

Mr O'Neil slipped three ten dollar notes into the slim black wallet which contained the bill before turning to give Malory a swift hug. "Knowing you, you've spent the last hour worried to death that I might be cross or disappointed in you for setting me up. I just want you to know that I'm neither."

The tension drained from Malory. "Mindreader . . . as usual," she admitted.

"But do me a favour. Next time you want to set me up with someone, try asking me first." Her dad spoke lightly but his blue eyes were serious. "Dating isn't the easiest idea for me to get my head around and I'm going to need more than a two second warning. OK?"

"OK," Malory agreed. She hesitated. "Does Matilda think I'm awful for what I did?"

"Au contraire." The corners of Carl O'Neil's mouth tugged up. "She thinks I have a wonderful daughter who is brave and kind enough to want me to be happy. And you know what?" He dropped a kiss on the top of her head. "She's right!"

The girls had arranged to go out for a trail ride the next day, keen to make the most of the crisp, dry weather. As she tacked up Tybalt, Malory kept running over the conversation with her father in her head. *Dad's still not ready to date*, she concluded. *He's not over Mom.* Tightening Tybalt's girth, she tried to work out how she felt. *Relieved*. There, she'd admitted it. Deep down she didn't want to share her father with anyone. If he was lonely then of course she would want him to have somebody else in his life. *But if he's happy with it being just the two of us, that suits me fine.*

Malory took hold of Tybalt's reins and led him out of his stall and down the centre aisle. Lani and Honey were outside the barn, already mounted, and moments later they heard the clopping of hooves against concrete as Dylan brought out Morello. "Talk about your fair-weather horse!" she complained. "He was determined not to come out in the cold so every time I tried to put the snaffle in his mouth he spat it out. Then he shook his head so hard the bridle flew into his bed and he wouldn't let me anywhere near it."

Malory couldn't help giggling at the image.

A grin broke out on Dylan's face. "I got the better of him by telling him there was a giant carrot walking down the aisle and when he went to look for it I rescued the bridle."

"You are such a terrible liar!" Honey groaned.

Dylan mounted. "OK, the truth is that I made a dive for it. I'd have been the butt of all of the horses' jokes if I'd let him get away with hiding his bridle from me!"

Lani's favourite pony, Colorado, started scraping the ground with his front hoof. "OK, boy, we're about to go!" Lani scolded him, lifting his head. The handsome dun-coloured pony tossed his head, puffing out his breath in a cloud.

"He might be cold," said Honey, through chattering teeth. She tugged at her scarf, pulling it up to cover her face. "I'll turn into an icicle if we don't get moving soon!"

They rode past the arenas in single file until the track widened enough to ride alongside each other. Tybalt suddenly broke into a trot and shot ahead of the others. Pulling him up, Malory leaned over to pat his neck. "It's OK, I know what you're thinking. It's totally the sort of weather that puts a tickle in your feet." Sunlight pooled on the frosty ground, making it sparkle like a carpet of crystals. Malory smiled at the romantic image as she shortened her reins. "Not too fast now, the ground's hard and I don't want you going lame," she warned

Tybalt. She called back over her shoulder, "How about a canter?"

When her friends agreed enthusiastically, she touched her heels to Tybalt's sides and sat deep in the saddle as he sprang into a smooth canter. She heard the others whoop as their horses followed Tybalt's lead. *Perfect*, Malory thought as they followed the trail, crunching over beds of fallen leaves and filling the woods with the sound of drumming hooves. When they finally pulled up, Malory was flushed from a mixture of cold and exhilaration. Tybalt snorted, his breath rising in a vapour.

"So," Dylan asked as she drew level with Malory, "how are you feeling now?"

"Better," Malory admitted. She hadn't been ready to discuss anything but the slightest details of her father's lunchtime date with Matilda before now. Dylan had been almost comically disappointed that Matilda was in a steady relationship already, but that wasn't the most important issue for Malory. She'd been doing a lot of thinking about how her dad must feel about beginning a new life so soon after her mum's death.

"I think that my dad just isn't ready to date yet," she confessed. "He's still not over my mom and, if I'm honest, I'm glad about that." She shot a sideways glance first at Dylan on one side and then at Lani and Honey on the other.

"I think I'd feel exactly the same if I were you," Dylan said frankly, taking Malory by surprise. "I can't imagine sharing my dad if he was left on his own."

"But you've been pushing for him and Matilda to get together," Malory said.

"Only because I thought that you were both ready for it," Dylan admitted. "If you're not, then you and your dad make a brilliant team as you are, so why do anything to break that up?"

Tybalt jogged on the spot and Malory automatically shortened her reins to control him, but in her mind she was mulling over what her friend had just said.

Dylan's right. There is no reason why I should try to change things. Dad and I are just fine on our own.

This week, Malory was looking forward to Tuesday even more than usual. Not only was their first equitation lesson scheduled during the afternoon, but afterwards there was an art exhibition in the school studio and her dad had agreed to come and view the collection with her.

Because of the persistently icy temperatures, their lesson was in the indoor arena and as Malory completed her warm-up she noticed a familiar figure walking into the upstairs viewing gallery. *Dad's early*, she thought, giving him a quick wave. She wondered if he'd arranged to get away from the store extra early so he could watch her ride.

Ali Carmichael looked to see who Malory had waved at. Spotting Mr O'Neil, she raised her hand before turning back to address the class. "Last week I asked you to research just what equitation is. Does anyone want to kick things off?"

Abigail called out, "It focuses on a rider's skills."

Ali Carmichael nodded. "Good. Can anyone elaborate?"

"The riders are assessed on their position and how effectively they control their horses," Honey put in.

"That's right. Equitation is all about riders being in total harmony with their horses no matter what gait they're in. When you're watching them, you should hardly be able to detect the aids they're giving to their horses," Ms Carmichael explained. "A lot of people are surprised when they find out that equitation classes include all different styles of riding, including dressage, showjumping and Western."

"Yes!" Lani whooped before leaning over to pat Colorado's neck. They had been the stars of a school rodeo held to raise funds for a local children's charity.

"But we're going to concentrate on what's known as hunt seat," Ms Carmichael continued, "in which you'll be learning not only to improve your position and control over a jumping course but also how well you maintain an even, forward pace and how accurately you judge the distance for each fence. Consistency is the key to success!"

Malory's heart sank a little. Her strength was that she rode instinctively and could get the best out of a horse by figuring out the best way to communicate what she wanted without challenging the horse's natural spirit, but finesse didn't top her skills list. *Unlike Lynsey.* She looked at the opposite side of the arena where Lynsey was sitting on Bluegrass with a smile tugging up the corners of her mouth. Malory turned her attention back to Tybalt who, for the first time since the start of term, had been working nicely on the bit, his neck nicely arched. *Tybalt's only consistency is his inconsistency!*

Ali Carmichael indicated the line of six jumps set down the middle of the arena. "I want you to ride through the grid thinking consistency, consistency, consistency. The fences are equally spaced apart and I'm looking for you to put in the same amount of strides between each one, with your take-off at the same distance each time. Your position must be controlled but relaxed. As you know, when your horses jump their centre of gravity moves forward because your horse is stretching out its head and neck. You need to move with the horse to make sure your weight is over the horse's centre of gravity. I want to see you folding forward at the hip, keeping your knees soft and your legs in the same position. I want to be able to draw an imaginary line through your shoulders, elbows, hips and ankles." She nodded at Lynsey to ride first. "None of what I've said is new, but we all tend to develop our own jumping styles that suit us and our horse. Equitation is about bringing you back to the classical style of riding and bringing out the best in you and your equine partner." She turned to watch Lynsey canter Bluegrass towards the grid. The roan's ears were pricked and his movement was supple as he sailed over the first of the fences. Lynsey sat perfectly still, following Bluegrass' movement as if they were one mythical creature, half-horse, half-girl.

"Excellent," Ms Carmichael pronounced as Lynsey finished the grid and trotted back to the group. "You held your position from beginning to end, the communication between you and Bluegrass was clear, and your aids were subtle." She looked at Dylan. "Off you go."

Morello cleared the first rail but misjudged the take-off point for the following fence. Launching himself into the air too early, his hind legs knocked the pole and he stumbled when he landed. The reins slipped through Dylan's fingers and she quickly gathered them as Morello put in two short strides and took off for the next fence, but he had got too close and rapped the pole with his front legs. For the remaining four rails, Morello got back into his stride and jumped clear. Dylan shook her head as she rode back to the group.

"What do you think went wrong to begin with?" Ali Carmichael asked her.

"I was so busy trying to get my own position perfect that I forgot all about Morello," Dylan admitted.

Ali Carmichael nodded. "Good equitation is all about communication between rider and horse." She glanced at Malory. "Ready?"

As Malory trotted Tybalt down the long side of the arena she mentally ran through everything she should be doing to achieve a perfect jumping position. She remembered Ali Carmichael's previous advice: *DAWNS. Don't look down, Always sit still, Weight into stirrups, Never break contact, Stay with your horse's movement.* She kept a steady contact on the reins as she turned Tybalt towards the line of jumps. With a whisk of his tail, Tybalt rose into the air and cleared the first fence, then put in two short strides and cleared the next.

Feeling him accelerate, Malory half halted. Tybalt got up too close to the third fence and Malory sat still to let him sort himself out instead of trying to interfere. Tybalt gave a leap almost from a standstill and as he landed Malory realized they'd need to put in an extra short stride to take off at the right point for the following fence. Closing her legs and sitting deep, she felt him bring his hindlegs well underneath. "Good boy," she murmured as he cleared the fence and went on to clear the final two as easily as the first.

"Top marks for helping Tybalt get through the grid without any knock-downs," Ali Carmichael congratulated her. "You reacted in exactly the right way. Unfortunately, as far as equitation goes you wouldn't have scored so highly."

Malory nodded. She needed to put in a lot of schooling to get Tybalt to work consistently. *He's no push button pony, that's for sure.* But he was responding to her commands now, which was an achievement that Malory rated on a par with any of Lynsey's A-Level circuit triumphs.

Once Malory had rubbed Tybalt down and rugged him she went in search of her father. "Dad!" she called when she spotted him talking to Ms Carmichael on the yard.

Her father finished what he was saying to the riding instructor before heading towards Malory with a wide smile on his face. "Ms Carmichael was just saying how you have a gift for bringing out the best in a horse. She puts Tybalt's progress down to the way you've handled him, getting him to put his trust in you."

"She said all that?" Malory felt her cheeks glow and it was nothing to do with the cold.

"Yup." Carl O'Neil put his arm around Malory's shoulders. "Do we have time for a hot drink before the exhibition?"

Malory nodded. "How about you go and get us a couple of hot chocolates while I get changed? I'll meet you over at the student centre in ten minutes."

Parting from her father where the footpath branched into different walkways, Malory raced back to Adams. She pulled on a clean pair of jeans, a purple sweater and her favourite Diesel jacket before hurrying to the student centre. Her father had chosen to sit on one of the brown leather sofas in the foyer in front of the glass windows.

"Thanks, Dad." Malory picked up her cup of hot chocolate from the coffee table. "This is great."

"Matilda asked me to say hi," he began, the corners of his mouth mischievously tugging up.

"She did?" Malory said carefully. "Is she OK?"

"Looking forward to Ashley coming home this weekend," Mr O'Neil told her. "She asked me if you'd begun your crafty club yet. I told her I thought you'd already held your first session last Saturday when you tried to set us up."

Malory winced. "You're never going to let me forget that are you?"

"Not for a long time, I'm afraid." Mr O'Neil grinned.

"It's not often you give me ammunition to tease you so I'm making the most of it."

"I didn't realize you had such a sadistic streak." Malory shook her head. "Matilda's well out of it!"

Her dad laughed. "Come on," he said, standing up. "Let's go see this exhibition."

As they made their way over to the Art Centre, Carl O'Neil said, "I was surprised to get your invite. I thought it was too early in term for an exhibition."

"The seniors have been working on individual projects since last year," Malory explained. "They were completed at the end of last term, and the exhibition was planned for the start of the new school term."

In front of the Art Centre was a sculpture of a large bronze prism with three benches angled around its base. Walking past it, they made their way into the foyer which had smaller sculptures on clear plastic stands. Malory led her father into the viewing gallery, where the seniors' work was on display in carefully lit rooms opening off the main walkway.

In the first room, Rachel Goodhart had sculpted a series of plates and mugs which had nature as their theme. Malory admired a platter in the shape of a giant leaf stained with autumnal colours.

"This is very good," Carl O'Neil said admiringly.

"Mr Woolley's an amazing teacher," Malory told him. "He's helping me work on a watercolour of Tybalt and he's given me some great advice."

"Your mom loved to paint," Carl O'Neil told her as he examined the handle of a cup which had been intricately fashioned into a daisy. "She once did an amazing seascape and gave it to me for an anniversary present."

"The one hanging in the hall?" Malory asked. She'd always thought it had been bought from a professional artist.

Her father nodded. "She was a woman of many talents," he said softly. "And her best talent of all was being a mother to you."

Malory felt a lump in her throat. How could she ever have thought that her father was ready to move on? *And how could I ever have thought I was ready to accept somebody else in Mom's place?*

After evening prep, Malory went to hand out the schedules she had printed detailing the term's practice sessions and competitions. "Can you make the first team practice on Saturday morning?" she asked as she handed the printed sheets to Lucy Price and Joanna Boardman, the seventh-grade members of the junior team.

"No worries," Lucy replied, "especially since there's under three weeks until the All Schools League competition."

"I hope we're going to be ready," Joanna said. "The opposition's pretty major."

"That's just what they're saying about us." Malory smiled. "Don't worry, we'll be ready to turn in our best performance yet."

Leaving them to examine their schedules, she headed to Lynsey's room and knocked on the door. When a voice called, "Yes?" Malory popped her head around and saw Lynsey and Patience sitting on Lynsey's bed. Lynsey glanced up from the music video they were watching on her iPad. "Dylan's not here," she said.

"It was you I came looking for." Malory walked into the room and held out the schedule. "I wanted to give you this."

Lynsey stood up and took the schedule. "I'm surprised you didn't laminate it," she commented as she ran her eye down the paper. "I would have done, if I'd been captain. A piece of paper like this could easily get scrunched up and thrown away by mistake."

Malory ignored the dig. "Will you be there on Saturday?"

Lynsey shrugged. "I'm the one person on the team who you don't have to stress over putting in an appearance. It's not like Blue and I need the practice."

"Maybe not, but your teammates need to practise with you," Malory said firmly. "It's important for morale that you're there."

"With Blue and me being in a whole different class from the rest of you, it's probably better for morale if I'm not there." Lynsey gave her a sugar-sweet smile. "And I'm sure it won't do your position as captain any favours if the rest of the team spend the whole session wondering why you've been given the place over me."

"Lynsey is the only rider on the team who's an A-Level circuit rider," Patience put in eagerly. "You can understand why it would be confusing for the rest of the team to be following you instead of her." She got up and brushed imaginary creases out of her Nocturne dress.

"You two are unbelievable." Dylan had walked into the room without Malory noticing. "Do you ever let up? Why can't you get the message that Malory's team captain because she deserves to be? I'd like to see you ride Tybalt and get the performance out of him that she can!"

"Whatever." Lynsey sounded bored as she pushed her feet into her Chloé boots. "As if I'd ever want to ride a horse that has clear mental issues." She shrugged. "But if one of the qualities of team captain is being a horse shrink, then I'll leave that to Malory and concentrate on perfecting my performance instead."

"I thought your performance was already perfect?" Dylan's voice was laced with sarcasm.

Lynsey hesitated and then smiled. "You know what? You're totally right. It is! So I don't see why Malory has to chase me down to try and force me into practice sessions I don't need." She glanced across at Patience. "Let's go to the student centre. I want to download Rihanna's latest video."

Dylan waited for Lynsey and Patience to leave before turning to Malory. Her cheeks were flushed as she fumed on behalf of her friend. "There's no way she'll risk her position on the team by not showing up for practice!" she exploded.

"I know." Malory suddenly felt weary. "But all this squabbling is no good for team spirit."

Dylan looked rueful. "I guess I was too quick to get

riled. Listen, I promise I'll try harder not to let her jibes get to me."

"Thanks." Malory nodded. "That would be a great help."

"There you go being all reasonable, proving yet again what a good decision Aunt Ali made by putting you in charge," Dylan said as she kicked off her shoes. "If it was me, I'd be making Lynsey eat hay by now."

Malory couldn't resist a smile at Dylan's description but her response was serious. "I owe so much to your aunt. I wouldn't have even got into Chestnut Hill without her backing. I have her to thank for everything."

She meant it, too. Ms Carmichael had been responsible for awarding Malory the prestigious scholarship that paid for her fees, as well as taking the risk of buying Tybalt when Malory spotted his potential at a dealer's yard. Malory respected all the staff at Chestnut Hill, but Ali was the only one she could ever say that she loved.

5

Arriving for team practice on Saturday morning, Malory halted just inside the arena and felt a rush of relief to see Lynsey cantering down the long side towards her.

"I told you," whispered Dylan, who had ridden in behind her. "There's no way she'll risk losing her place on the team."

There was a clatter of hooves as Lucy and Joanna rode up to the entrance. "Are we spectating or riding today?" Joanna called out cheerfully.

Malory rode Tybalt forward and began to ride a serpentine. Tybalt arched his neck and his stride became steadier and more powerful as he brought his hindquarters underneath him.

"Good boy," Malory murmured. She was pleased at the way Tybalt was beginning to come back into condition after his holiday. Out of the corner of her eye, she could see Bluegrass doing a perfect flying change. The roan looked amazing as he cantered calmly across the diagonal. Even though it was just a practice session,

Lynsey was immaculately turned out in polished leather boots, oatmeal jodhpurs and team sweatshirt.

"Lucy!" Ali Carmichael called. "Your reins are too long and you're sitting too far forward so the energy you're creating with your legs is wasted. If you don't maintain contact with Skylark's mouth, you can't contain her movement and her weight will fall on to her forehand. Don't forget that how you start off can set up your horse's attitude to the entire training session. So don't get sloppy!"

Malory transferred a hundred-per-cent attention to Tybalt until Ms Carmichael called a halt to the warm-up session. "The jumps set out are those that have caused problems in the past." She pointed to the four jumps at the bottom half of the arena.

"Bluegrass and I haven't had any problems," Lynsey chipped in.

"Thank you, Lynsey. I'm addressing the team, not individuals," Ali Carmichael said crisply.

"You mean we're not going over the full course?" Lynsey pointed to the set of eight jumps at the opposite end of the arena.

"They're for the senior practice. Malory, why don't you go first?" Ms Carmichael suggested.

Malory nodded and rode Tybalt away from the group.

"You can see that Malory's got Tybalt working well. His hind legs are active, his strides even and he's holding a good outline," Ms Carmichael commented as Malory cantered Tybalt towards the first fence. "Malory's keeping a steady contact and a light seat. She's absorbing Tybalt's movement with her hips and back and this is all helping to set him up nicely."

Malory concentrated on the centre of the parallel bars as she squeezed her legs to keep Tybalt going in a straight line. "Watch how Malory closes down the angles at her hip, knee and ankle." Ms Carmichael's voice carried over as Tybalt gathered himself and rose into the air. "Tybalt's looking alert in response to Mal's positive signals."

Tybalt landed clear and cantered around the corner to the next fence. Malory kept her legs on so he didn't lose any impulsion. Realizing that Tybalt was leading with the wrong leg, she slipped her outside leg back and pressed hard while shifting her weight to the inside of the saddle. Tybalt responded with a flying change, switching legs mid-stride in a movement that felt like he was skipping.

"Well handled!" Ms Carmichael called approvingly.

Tybalt sailed over the wall before cantering steadily on to the double. The first element was an upright and Malory half halted as Tybalt snatched at the bit and tried to rush at the fence. The moment they landed, she sat upright to set the gelding up for the second element. She used her legs and Tybalt's stride lengthened to get close to the spread. Malory felt a rush of pride as Tybalt cleared it easily. "Clever boy." She patted his shoulder as they cantered back to the rest of the team.

"Well done!" Ms Carmichael exclaimed. "You rode that pitch perfect." Malory saw Dylan shoot Lynsey a look that said "beat that".

"OK, Lucy, off you go," Ms Carmichael said.

Lucy trotted Skylark in a circle before facing the first jump. Skylark's movement flattened as he sped up, and he hurtled over the fence, knocking off the top pole.

"Bring him back and try again," Ms Carmichael instructed as she hurried over to put the pole back into place. "Malory, can you tell Lucy why she had a knock-down?"

"You allowed Skylark to try and get over using speed instead of impulsion," Malory told the seventh-grader. "He lost his outline and rhythm, and you dropped all contact when you felt him going too fast instead of collecting him."

Ms Carmichael nodded as she walked away from the fence. "Try again, but this time keep contact with your legs and hands."

Lucy rode at the fence again and this time sat deep and kept contact on the reins. Skylark pricked his ears and sailed over the fence.

"Much better!" Ms Carmichael called.

Lynsey let out a sigh as Lucy rode towards the next fence. "If I'd known this was going to be a kindergarten practice session, I'd have stayed in bed," she muttered. The irritation etched on her face transferred to Bluegrass, who swished his tail and took two steps back.

Why can't Lynsey get her head around the fact that being part of a team means supporting one another? Turning her attention back to Lucy, Malory clapped as she landed clear of the double.

"OK, Dylan. Let's see if we can work on Morello's dislike of fences out of corners," Ms Carmichael suggested.

"Why don't we just strap stabilizers on him and have done with it?" Lynsey muttered as Morello trotted away. Malory wondered whether it was worth trying to give Lynsey a team pep talk but abandoned the idea as one that would crash and burn.

"Don't forget to use your weight when you land after the parallel to tell Morello what leg to lead off on," Ms Carmichael reminded Dylan. "Then use your legs to get his hindquarters engaged. Keep thinking balance and remaining upright and remember to keep Morello correctly aligned. If only fifty per cent of Morello's energy is aiming straight at the fence then he only has fifty per cent power to jump properly. Fences out of corners don't all have to be bogeys for Morello, I promise!"

Lynsey trotted Bluegrass away with another exclamation of annoyance. With a sinking feeling, Malory realized she was abandoning the training session. Ms Carmichael had her back turned and Malory wondered if she could possibly ride after Lynsey and get her to come back before the instructor noticed what was going on. But Dylan was approaching the final fence, so there was no time.

As Morello landed clear, Ms Carmichael turned back to the rest of the group. Her eyes narrowed as she looked past them farther down the school. As Malory followed the instructor's gaze, she heard Joanna gasp. Malory shook her head in disbelief as she watched Lynsey sail over an upright on the seniors' practice course. *What is her problem?*

Ms Carmichael remained silent while Lynsey and Bluegrass completed the remaining five fences. Bluegrass' eyes were bright and his ears pricked as he tackled each fence. As they landed clear of the treble, Lynsey cantered back down the arena looking smug.

"Bluegrass flattened when he saw the final element of the treble," Ms Carmichael said evenly, "which shows that even the most polished horses can be surprised by a fence. Because of his experience, he was able to make up the extra ground after landing short. If it hadn't been for him rescuing you both, you would have landed in the middle of the fence."

Lynsey's smile faded.

"Maybe we can add a treble to our next practice session over fences we've all had trouble with," Dylan suggested, straight-faced.

"For now I think your horses have all done more than enough and deserve to be cooled down." Ms Carmichael's tone was calm but Malory could tell by the tight line of her mouth that she was angry with Lynsey.

Feeling troubled, Malory let Tybalt cool off by walking him on a loose rein before taking him back to his stall. "I bet you'd be able to whip the team into shape if you were captain, huh?" she murmured, leaning against the gelding's shoulder. Tybalt looked around at her and nosed hopefully at her pocket. "You'd know how to deal with Lynsey."

"Lynsey doesn't need dealing with. She needs exterminating," came a cheerful voice.

"Tybalt, that's no way to talk about a member of the team," Malory said sternly. Without turning around, she continued, "Hi, Dylan."

"That was some practice session, huh?" Dylan came into the stall. "How Aunt Ali didn't bust something when Lynsey rode over the seniors' course, I'll never know."

"She is sailing close to the wind," Malory agreed, thinking of Lynsey's array of sarcastic comments. She fiddled with a strand of Tybalt's mane. "I don't know what to do. I feel like I should be able to do something about her since I'm team captain, but I can't help feeling that it's *because* I'm captain that she's doing it."

"Well, I hope you're not going to suggest stepping down," Dylan told her, "because if you did that I'd have to spike Bluegrass' water to stop Lynsey muscling in on your place."

"We can't have that," Malory said ruefully. "He's the best horse on the team. Apart from Tybalt of course."

"And Morello," Dylan said in mock outrage.

Malory suddenly burst out laughing. "Could you imagine Lynsey placing Bluegrass below Tybalt and Morello? If she had her way they wouldn't even be on the team."

"Which is one very good reason why she's not making the decisions around here," Dylan pointed out. "And talking of decisions, are you ready to go over to the student centre for a hot drink?"

Malory nodded. Her hands and feet felt like blocks of

ice, and she couldn't think of anything better to defrost them than a mug of hot chocolate. "I wish all choices were so easy!" she said wistfully.

In Monday's art class, Malory selected a fine sable brush and carefully added a black outline around Tybalt's large intelligent eyes before sitting back to examine the painting. "I think I'm done," she announced. She had copied the photograph Dylan had given her for Christmas, and was delighted with the results.

Lani came over to admire the picture. "That's so lifelike it looks as if he's about to jump right off the paper."

"Thanks," Malory said. "I think I'm going to send it to my dad." She felt a rush of emotion at the thought of it hanging alongside her mother's picture. Her mom would have been so proud to know that Malory loved painting, too. She looked up and noticed that Lani's hands and cheeks were speckled with multicoloured dabs of paint. "You look as if you've been wrestling with your paint palette," she commented.

Lani stared ruefully at her hands. "I can never figure how it gets everywhere. There's more on me than there is on the paper." She shrugged. "Although the way I paint, that's no bad thing."

"Your picture of Colorado's coming on well," Malory said loyally.

"Hah! It looks as if he's run into a giant marshmallow and is trying to fight his way free!" Lani went back to her easel as Mr Woolley came over to look at Malory's picture.

"Great work, Malory," he said. "I wouldn't do

anything more on it now. Let it dry, and then I'd like to include it in the exhibition over at the Old House."

Malory felt her cheeks go pink. Only a few students' work was selected each year to go on display at the Old House. It was a huge honour. But she'd already made up her mind what she was going to do with this picture. Regretfully she shook her head. "That would be amazing but if it's OK, I'd rather send it to my dad."

Mr Woolley smiled. "Our loss is your father's gain! Would you like me to wrap it up for you once it's dry?"

"That would be great," Malory said as the art teacher lifted her board with the painting taped to it. She glanced at her watch and saw that there was just enough time left in the lesson to include a note to her father in the parcel. Taking a pen and her notebook from her bag, she began to write.

Hi Dad,

I know, I know, you're probably thinking that even though I'm back in school you can't seem to get rid of me! Here's the painting I was telling you about – I thought you might like to hang it in the hall alongside Mom's. Doesn't Tybalt look gorgeous?

It was really great seeing you the other day. One of the nicest things about being at school is that you're close by. I hope we can get together again soon – just us, I promise!

Take care and tonnes of love and kisses,

Mal xx

Folding up the piece of paper Malory took it to Mr Woolley, who was mixing paints. "Could you put this in with the painting?" she asked, handing over the note.

"No problem," Mr Woolley said. He wiped his hands on a cloth and took the folded paper "Let me know what your dad thinks of the painting."

"Sure thing," Malory promised, although she already knew that her father would be thrilled. He still had the very first crayon drawing she had scribbled when she was one year old! She blinked as she realized that her mom would have seen that drawing, too. *I hope you can see this one, Mom.*

Malory stayed in her room on Wednesday evening instead of going down to the common room. She hadn't finished all of her work during prep and was trying to cram for a Biology test. She stared at the diagram of two plants and tried to recall different types of pollination. "Insect pollination, self-pollination. . ." she muttered, breaking off as someone knocked at the door.

"There's a call for you downstairs," Razina called.

"Thanks. I'm just coming." Malory pushed her chair back from her desk. Knowing that Mr Woolley had posted the painting, she wasn't surprised to hear her father on the other end of the phone.

"It's wonderful, I love it!" Carl O'Neil told her. "I've been showing it to every customer who's come into the shop today!" Malory felt her cheeks get hot. "Your mom would have been bursting with pride," her dad added softly. "Our amazing, talented daughter. I've just finished hanging it in the hall alongside your mom's picture. Every visitor is going to have to admire them equally before being allowed entry, starting with Matilda and Ashley this evening!"

"Ashley's home?" Malory felt a sense of relief that they could discuss Matilda without any awkwardness.

"He's on leave for a few days," Mr O'Neil told her. "They're bringing Chinese takeout and we're going to play Trivial Pursuit."

"Well, if you get any questions on plant reproduction, call me," Malory told him with a laugh. "I've got a Biology test tomorrow."

"I'll let you get back to your revision, then," Mr O'Neil said. "Thanks again for the painting."

"You're welcome," Malory told him before hanging up. As she headed back to her room she felt a glow of happiness; underlying it was a sense of relief that her matchmaking efforts hadn't done anything to spoil their relationship. *He's my best friend as well as being my dad,* she thought. *And I never want to do anything to mess that up.*

The next morning Malory resisted the temptation to take out her Biology revision notes at breakfast. Opposite her Dylan was running her finger down her notebook.

"If you don't know it now. . ." Lani warned, shaking her head.

Dylan looked up, her red hair sticking up as she pushed her hand through it. "It's OK for you, given that you have a bionic memory for facts and figures. There's no point for me in revising until the very last moment because the info only sticks around for a few hours before emptying right out again."

"Thank goodness you don't have the same problem remembering which order to jump fences," Malory told her.

"Or which movements to make in a dressage test," Honey added.

"That's different, I enjoy those," Dylan said as she dropped her gaze back to her book.

"Yeah well, you know I struggle with remembering dressage letters." Lani was determined not to be outdone. "Something's got to be logical for my memory to kick in."

"Talking of riding," Malory murmured, looking over at the canteen doors. Ms Carmichael was standing just inside the entrance, scanning the room.

"Who do you think she's looking for?" Honey said.

Dylan turned in her seat. "Wow, her new hairdo totally rocks. I can't remember the last time she had it styled."

Malory had to admit that the way their instructor's hair had been shaped with layers and a fringe to frame her face really suited her. Maybe she'd had it cut to fit more comfortably under a riding helmet. "But she doesn't look happy," she commented, checking out Ali Carmichael's frown.

"You haven't been taking part in any more midnight rides, have you, Dyl?" Lani said as Ms Carmichael began to head their way.

Malory's stomach churned as it occurred to her something might have happened to Tybalt but then she noticed Ali Carmichael's gaze was fixed to the left of them.

Lynsey and Patience! Malory looked at the others and saw that they had already come to the same conclusion.

"Lynsey?" Ms Carmichael's voice rang out.

Lynsey looked up from the fashion magazine she was reading while eating a fruit salad. Her fork paused halfway to her mouth. "Yes?"

"I need you to come down to the barn right away."

Lynsey lowered her fork. "Why? What's wrong?"

Sympathy filled Ali Carmichael's blue eyes. "I'm sorry, but Bluegrass has injured himself. It's fairly serious, I'm afraid."

6

Lynsey pushed back her chair, her face suddenly white. "What happened?"

"He was lame when Kelly went to turn him out this morning," Ms Carmichael told her. "He might have hurt himself in his stall during the night. There's heat and swelling in his off hind, and he's clearly in a lot of pain so I've put an emergency call out to the vet."

Patience's hand flew up to cover her mouth and as Lynsey rushed out of the canteen she quickly followed.

"This is not good," Dylan said soberly.

Malory bit her lower lip. "I'm going to head down to the yard as soon as I've finished breakfast."

Honey shot her a sympathetic glance. "Are you worried about the team?"

Malory nodded. Her first concern was for Bluegrass, and for Lynsey who adored her talented pony, but as team captain she also had the whole team's performance to think about. If Bluegrass was out of action it would be bad news for them all, especially with the next All Schools League competition just around the corner.

She glanced down at her half-eaten bowl of granola and couldn't raise the appetite to finish it. "I'm out of here," she said. With half an hour to go before classes began, she just had enough time to check on Bluegrass.

The others caught up with her as she was walking down to the yard. The grass on each side of the path was crisp with frost, and around them the branches of the trees were delicately outlined with silver. Without any leaves on the trees, the view of the yard was unobscured.

Honey pointed at the jeep parked in front of the barn's white double doors. "Dr Olton's here."

Inside the barn, Kelly and Patience were looking over Blue's door. Malory and the others squeezed up beside them and gazed over the half wall at the gelding. Bluegrass was balancing on three legs, his coat damp with sweat as he trembled with pain and shock. Malory was startled by how different he looked from the poised, impeccably-schooled jumper in the show ring. Lynsey and Ali Carmichael stood on either side of his head while Dr Olton gently ran her hand down his hind leg. Lynsey was holding Bluegrass' leather headcollar and murmuring gently to him. *He looks scared*. Malory felt a rush of sympathy for the beautiful roan. The whites of his eyes showed and he shifted restlessly as Dr Olton pressed on the inflamed area.

"Steady, Blue," Lynsey soothed. "Stand still, it'll be over soon."

Dr Olton straightened up and patted Bluegrass' shoulder. "Take it easy, there's a good boy."

"What's wrong with him?" Lynsey's voice was high with anxiety.

"He's taken a knock to his fetlock and he's going to need complete rest to let the swelling go down, I'm afraid. I'll arrange for his leg to be X-rayed so we can work out what the exact damage is but I suspect he's going to be out of action for some time."

Patience's eyes were wide. "How could he have got hurt?"

Dr Olton hesitated. "It's difficult to say. The most likely explanation is that he's kicked himself in his stall, maybe when rolling." She reached down to open her case. "I'm going to give him a course of anti-inflammatories and an injection for the pain, and both hind legs will need to be bandaged for support."

Lynsey took the sachets of powders from the vet. "Is he in much pain?" She turned back to Bluegrass and slipped her arm around his neck. Malory felt a stab of pity for Lynsey. No matter how difficult she was at times, no one could doubt how much she loved Bluegrass.

"He's going to be feeling very sorry for himself, but we'll get him sorted asap," Dr Olton told her.

"I want my own vet to take a look at him." Lynsey spoke abruptly to Ms Carmichael.

"I'm sure all your vet will do is back up what Dr Olton has already told you," Ali Carmichael said quietly.

"I can send the X-rays over to your vet if you'd like," Dr Olton said as she snapped her case shut.

Lynsey nodded. "As soon as you've taken them please, I'll phone ahead to tell him what's happening."

As Lynsey fished her phone out of her pocket, Ali Carmichael glanced over at Malory and the others. "You'd all better get going or you'll be late for class."

"I'm really sorry about Bluegrass," Malory told Lynsey.

"Thanks," she replied briefly, putting her phone to her ear.

Malory sighed as they walked out of the barn. "This really sucks."

"It sure does. I've never seen Lynsey look so freaked out," Dylan commented.

"That's nothing compared with how much she'll freak out later," Patience said from behind them.

Malory turned around and stared at her.

"Well, she'll want to find out just how Bluegrass got hurt," Patience went on, pulling her woollen cap further down. "Someone's got to take the blame for this."

"Quit stirring things up," Lani advised. "Accidents happen."

Patience shrugged. "I doubt Lynsey's going to see it that way." As she walked by, Malory realized that at least some of what Patience had said was true. Lynsey wasn't going to be happy about Bluegrass being out of action.

"I see stormy times ahead," Dylan commented, which pretty much summed up Malory's thoughts exactly.

"Excusez moi, Malory." Mme Dubois' husky voice interrupted Malory and Dylan's whispered conversation.

"I'm sure what you have to say is of tremendous interest since you feel the need to discuss it during class. Why don't you let us all in on your, how do you say, 'hot goss'?"

Malory felt her face burn as she met her French teacher's gaze. "We were just talking about Bluegrass," she explained.

"Bluegrass? The perfume?" Mme Dubois' voice rose.

"No." Malory shifted uncomfortably in her seat as giggles broke out around the classroom. "Lynsey's horse. He's injured himself."

"Ah, now I see. And you are so concerned because you are Lynsey's great friend and captain of the junior team?" Mme Dubois nodded. "You must feel free to continue your conversation with Dylan, of course." She paused. "Mais en français, s'il vous plaît."

Dylan turned pale. "Um, if it's OK maybe we could finish it during recess?" she suggested.

Mme Dubois dipped her head. "Just so. Perhaps I might recommend that all conversations you cannot translate into French are reserved for recess from now on." She raised her eyebrows pointedly. "Now class, if you would look at the whiteboard and repeat the following after me." She indicated the first line of vocabulary and Malory began to chant the words along with everyone else, but it was impossible to concentrate. Her thoughts kept straying to poor Bluegrass and Lynsey, and just what the repercussions were going to be for the junior team.

*

Bluegrass lifted his head as Malory and Dylan looked over his wall. His eyes, which were usually so bright and alert, were dull.

"Lie still, Blue." Lynsey stroked the roan's neck from where she sat beside him. With a heavy sigh, Bluegrass settled his head back against the straw.

"How is he?" Malory asked. She felt Honey and Lani crowd up behind her.

"It's the worst news." Lynsey's eyes were red rimmed. "He's got a hairline fracture of his fetlock and he needs total rest. He's going to be out of action for weeks."

Malory glanced at Bluegrass' heavily bandaged hindleg. "Poor Blue," she said softly.

Lynsey was silent as she brushed her fingers down Bluegrass' cheek. Then she looked hard at Malory. "Or do you mean poor you?"

Malory frowned. "Huh?"

"You've just lost the best horse on the team. You're not exactly going to go down as the most successful captain in school history now you don't have Blue to carry you."

Malory caught her breath at Lynsey's cheap jibe. *She has to be kidding; she can't really think that all I care about is how this is going to reflect on me?* But she couldn't help feeling uncomfortable as she recalled the way she and Dylan had joked about where Bluegrass ranked on the team.

"You're unbelievable!" Dylan exclaimed. "Is there ever going to be a time when you can resist having a dig? Maybe the fact that you took Bluegrass over a course that was too demanding has something to do with his injury. And if you ask me it's Mal who does the carrying, especially when you do your best to trash team practices which aren't going your way."

"I wasn't asking you," Lynsey snapped. "The main reason being because whenever you open your mouth I'm in danger of Death by Boredom."

"Time out, guys," Lani interrupted. "The last thing Bluegrass needs is stressing out."

"I agree," Ali Carmichael said as she walked into the barn. "I could hear your voices out on the yard. I don't know what you're arguing about and I don't want to know. I do however want to do everything I can to help Bluegrass' recovery and if that means asking you all to clear out then that's exactly what I'll do." Her blue eyes regarded them coolly.

Honey slipped her arm through Dylan's. "Come on, let's go make a start on the tack cleaning."

Dylan glanced at Malory. "Are you coming?"

"I'd like a word with Malory. She can join up with you in a couple of minutes." Ms Carmichael waited for the girls to leave before looking at Malory. "I'm sure you're aware that we can substitute another horse in Blue's place for the All Schools League." Malory nodded; it was the riders who made up the team, not their horses. Ali Carmichael turned to include Lynsey in the conversation. "I think you should ride Knight's Quest in Blue's place for the next few weeks, Lynsey. I know it won't be the same as riding Bluegrass, but you're a talented rider and Quest is an experienced show horse with excellent jumping credentials. If you work hard to develop a rapport with him between now and the competition, I'm confident you'll turn in a great performance."

A muscle jumped in Lynsey's jaw and when she didn't say anything, Ms Carmichael went on reassuringly, "I'll be back to check on Blue soon so don't feel you have to spend the whole evening out here, although I can see he's glad to have you with him."

After their instructor had left Malory said, "I'm sure you and Quest will make great partners." The note of brightness in her voice sounded forced, even to her ears.

Lynsey bowed her head and ignored Malory's comment.

With a sigh, Malory turned away from the stall door, but not before she'd seen a tear fall from Lynsey's cheek on to Bluegrass' neck.

"Hey, Mal, are you ready?" Dylan stepped out into the dorm corridor at the same time as Malory. "We owe Honey and Lani a re-match."

Malory waited for Dylan to lock her door. The previous night they'd been beaten two out of three games of ping pong, and Dylan was determined to win second time around. "I'm just going to give my dad a quick call first," Malory told her.

Parting from Dylan outside the common room, she headed down to the foyer. The elaborate glass chandelier had been switched off, leaving two ginger jar lamps filling the hall with a warm glow. Kathryn MacIntyre was using the phone so Malory sat down at a coffee table to wait. Picking up a magazine, she flicked idly through the pages and noticed a template for a homemade Valentine card, using scarlet ribbon and tiny crystals. *This could be just the project to kick start Get Crafty*, she thought, deciding to make photocopies of it in the morning. She'd forgotten how close it was to Valentine's Day. She liked the idea of sending a card to Caleb – although she'd write something jokey inside so he wouldn't feel embarrassed if he opened it in front of his friends.

"I'm all done, Mal," Kathryn called as she hung up.

"Thanks." Malory made her way over to the phone and picked up the receiver.

"Hey, hon," her father said warmly when he answered. "I didn't expect to hear from you so soon."

Malory detected a faint note of concern under his words. "It hasn't been the best of days and I wanted to hear your voice," she admitted.

"You're worried about Lynsey's horse's injury," Carl O'Neil guessed.

Malory blinked. "How did you know about that?"

"Bad news travels fast," her father told her. "You must be concerned for the team."

Malory hesitated. "The most important thing is that Bluegrass gets better but yes, I can't help wondering what's going to happen to the team now."

"Lynsey will be teamed up with another horse though, right?" Carl O'Neil said.

Malory smiled. "So something of what I tell you about competition rules must hit the mark."

"I always listen to what you say," Mr O'Neil responded.

"I must be mistaking the glazed look that comes into your eyes whenever I talk horse," Malory teased.

"Now you know it's one of intense concentration." Her father's voice caught with laughter. "So now that you can rest assured that you're speaking to someone knowledgeable, you can trust me when I say that the team isn't just Bluegrass. Sure he's one talented horse, but so are all of the rest."

"I'm mostly worried about team morale," Malory confessed. "How do I convince everyone we can still do well in the All Schools League competition when I'm not a hundred-per-cent sure myself?"

"The way I see it, you need to start believing in yourself a little more." Mr O'Neil sounded thoughtful. "The rest of the team need to see that you still have total confidence in them. Being able to show them that, even when you're wrestling with your own doubts, is what makes a great leader. And I know you're a great leader."

Malory took a deep breath. "Thanks, Dad. I needed that."

"Any time," Carl O'Neil told her. "Now, as much as I love talking I'm sure you've got far more interesting things to do than spending your free time on the other end of the phone to me."

"I do have a ping pong re-match to win," Malory admitted.

"Ah, that's the kind of fighting spirit I like to hear," her father cheered.

"Nothing else from here on in," Malory responded. "And that's a promise!"

7

"Do you think Lynsey's going to show?" Dylan asked Malory as they rode towards the indoor arena.

"It's Lynsey, so who knows?" Malory replied. The main reason for calling the Sunday afternoon team practice had been for Lynsey, who had spent the entire weekend in Blue's stall. "With the competition next Saturday, she's got less than a week to get to know Quest." Riding into the arena, she felt a rush of relief when she spotted Lynsey warming up the big grey gelding at the far end.

"So far so good," Dylan murmured before dropping behind Tybalt.

As she worked Tybalt, Malory kept an eye on Lynsey and was reassured to see Quest responding obediently to her. Joanna rode in on Calvin, closely followed by Lucy who also threw curious glances at Lynsey to see how she was getting on with her new ride.

Ali Carmichael had set out a canter grid of four uprights and one parallel along the centre line. She stood to one side of the fences and waited for the girls to finish warming up before calling them in.

"Thanks for making it to this afternoon's training session," she said. "I know Malory's arranged a few extra practices due to Bluegrass being out of action and it's important you make them all if you can."

Malory noticed Lynsey's leather gloved hands twitch on the reins. Quest's quarters swung out and with a click of impatience Lynsey nudged him back in line.

"I think it's best if you take Quest through the grid first so we can see how the two of you go," Ali Carmichael suggested.

With a brief nod Lynsey circled Quest away from the group and set the dappled grey into a canter. As they headed at the first of the fences, Malory saw that instead of being supple and relaxed in the saddle Lynsey had lines of tension running through her. *Her arms are stiff*, she noted as Quest threw up his head in protest. The gelding picked up his pace as he rushed the fence and lost his straight approach. The next fence Quest rattled with his forelegs and Lynsey responded by tapping him with her whip. Flattening his ears, Quest refused the third upright and Lynsey rode him back to Ali Carmichael with her cheeks flushed.

"He's useless," she announced.

"Quest's far from useless," Ali Carmichael responded calmly. "But he's not a push button horse, either. He's one of the best jumpers on the yard but he's a real thinker and expects his partner to put in as much effort as he's being asked for. He's not going to do anything automatically for you and the moment you stop riding sympathetically he's going to dig his heels in."

"It sounds like he needs a shrink, not a rider." Lynsey's tone was loaded with disgust.

Ali Carmichael sighed. "OK, I guess you need some time to adjust to a different horse's personality so let's just concentrate for now on the specifics of what went wrong. Quest wasn't properly balanced on his approach to the grid. He ended up drifting through his right shoulder. If you had circled him a few times until you were both settled then you would have put in a different performance."

Lynsey's flush deepened and Malory shot her a sympathetic glance. *I'd find it so hard if Tybalt was injured and suddenly taken away from me.* She leaned forward to stroke the gelding's satiny neck.

"Malory, how about you give Lynsey a lead through the grid?" Ms Carmichael suggested.

"I don't need a lead," Lynsey objected. "I just need a horse that's on the same level as I am."

"OK, quit your stirrups and jump off," Ms Carmichael told her. "You too, Malory."

With a jolt of surprise Malory slid down from Tybalt. Ali Carmichael walked over and took Tybalt's reins. "I'd like you to take Quest through the grid," she told her.

Malory looked uncertainly at the dappled gelding. How would Lynsey feel if she got on with Quest more successfully than she had done?

"The reason I'm asking Malory to take Quest over the fences is to give you a chance to examine his style," Ali Carmichael told Lynsey, as if she'd read Malory's mind.

Feeling slightly more comfortable, Malory walked over to take Quest's reins. She swung up into the saddle and adjusted her stirrups before nudging Quest forward. The gelding's stride was long and eager. His ear flicked back and, forgetting that she was being watched, Malory talked out loud to him.

"I bet you're wondering who's on your back now, huh? Well, I'll cut you a deal, we won't do anything until you're ready, but then you've got to give me a hundred per cent, OK?" She kept a gentle but firm pressure with her legs, letting Quest know that she was confident they could get the job done. Increasing the pressure, she sent the gelding into a canter around the arena and then into a twenty-metre circle until she felt him settle. When they turned towards the row of fences, Malory concentrated on keeping Quest balanced. She held him in until the last minute, and when she let him go one stride away, she caught her breath at the surge of power from his hindquarters. Keeping her eyes on the next fence, she counted two strides before nudging him to take off. With a snort, Quest folded his forelegs neatly and cleared the rail with inches to spare.

"Good boy!" Malory called. At the last fence, she kept her legs on while keeping hold of the reins to encourage him to put in a short stride. With his weight on his haunches, Quest had all the power he needed to make the spread and Malory couldn't help grinning as they flew over the coloured poles. Quest gave a small buck after the fence and Malory patted his shoulder, laughing at his high spirits.

"Way to go!" Ali Carmichael called as Malory circled and brought Quest back to the line. Her excitement died away when Lynsey refused to meet her eye. Slipping down from the saddle, Malory patted the gelding one last time before handing over the reins. "He's lovely." She struggled to find the right words. "But I get the feeling he likes to keep a dialogue going."

"Gee, thanks for the lesson, Mal." Lynsey's voice was icy.

Malory froze. The last thing she'd wanted was to sound patronizing.

Quest snorted and tossed his head as Lynsey gathered up the reins. "Did that help at all?" Ali Carmichael asked as Lynsey mounted.

Lynsey shrugged. "He's no Bluegrass."

Malory felt a surge of irritation as she reclaimed Tybalt. No one could blame Lynsey for wishing Quest was Bluegrass but it wasn't helpful that she seemed determined to resent everything about her new horse. Now was the time to be moving forward and getting the team back on track.

"Anything else?" Ali Carmichael's tone was even.

"I guess he's got some style," Lynsey said grudgingly. "But that's no good if he switches it off and on." Without waiting for Ms Carmichael's signal, she rode Quest away from the group and pushed him into a canter.

Malory willed the gelding to go well for Lynsey as they headed towards the grid. Quest's ears pricked forward and he stood well back on his hocks to take the first fence. As soon as they landed Lynsey seemed to lose concentration and looked down. She tipped forward in the saddle and as the next jump loomed she was in front of Quest's movement.

Malory's heart sank as Lynsey lost her rein contact. Quest rushed the next fence and brought it down with his hindlegs. Malory glanced at Dylan, whose green eyes mirrored her own concern.

"This is so not Lynsey," Joanna whispered on Malory's other side.

"It's so not Quest either," Malory murmured as Quest tipped the final fence with his forelegs. *This isn't good.* If Lynsey couldn't get over her distress at being parted from Bluegrass, the entire team would end up paying.

After the practice, Malory cross-tied Tybalt outside his stall to sponge off his sweat marks. Setting down a bucket of water, she patted his neck before going to fetch a sweat scraper. A loud clatter made her spin around to see the bucket skid across the aisle and strike Tybalt's hindleg. Water flooded over the floor and into the side gutter as Tybalt threw up his head in fright. His hooves clattered on the concrete and his shoes left skid marks across the pale stone.

"I'm sorry!" Abigail cried. "I didn't see the bucket." The seventh-grader was standing in the door of the nearest stall looking utterly dismayed, and soaked up to her knees.

Tybalt danced on the spot, striking the bucket again. The whites of his eyes showed as he strained against his lead ropes. "Whoa, Tyb. Steady boy." Malory lifted the bucket out of the way and moved forward to calm him. As she reached out to grasp his headcollar, Tybalt plunged forward. To her alarm, Malory saw the headcollar's buckle rip from its lining, and the halter dropped uselessly to the ground. Just as Tybalt shook himself free, Malory grabbed his mane and led him into his stall before he could escape down the aisle. She checked his hindlegs to make sure he hadn't injured himself, then ran her hand soothingly down his neck. "You're fine," she reassured him.

"Wow, fast reaction." Abigail handed her the broken headcollar as she came out of Tybalt's stall. "If you hadn't caught him, he'd have been on his way out of here."

"Thanks. I'd better go and get another," Malory told her.

At the end of the aisle, Ali Carmichael was looking over the door of Blue's stall.

"How is he?" Malory asked.

Ms Carmichael leaned her arms on top of the door. "He seems a little brighter today."

Bluegrass was standing in the middle of his stall, balancing his weight on his good legs while resting his injured hind. Malory felt relieved to see his dark eyes were more alert. "Lynsey will be pleased to see him looking a bit better."

Ali Carmichael nodded as she drew back the lock on the stall door.

"Tybalt just broke his headcollar," Malory said, holding up the broken halter. "He got startled when he was side tied."

Ali Carmichael turned around and examined the nylon strap. She clicked with annoyance. "This shouldn't have broken like that." Glancing up, she shot Malory a concerned look. "You didn't get hurt?"

Malory shook her head. "I'm fine," she assured her instructor. "I was going to go and get another from the tack room."

"I had half a dozen new ones delivered yesterday," Ali Carmichael told her. "They're in my kitchen waiting to be taken out of their packaging. Do you mind going to get one of those? I want to check all the old ones to make sure they're not about to break, too."

"Sure," Malory agreed.

"The back door's open. Just go straight in," Ali Carmichael said.

As she stepped out of the barn and took a mouthful of icy air, Malory tugged up the zip on her riding jacket. She couldn't believe it could be this cold without snowing! She headed off the yard and took the narrow gravel path to Ali Carmichael's cottage, which sat cosily behind the barns. Light spilled out of the windows, bathing the front garden in a warm yellow glow. Even though it was winter, plants with delicate white flowers spilled over the edges of the window boxes, and a pretty clipped box tree stood in a terracotta pot beside the front door.

Malory walked around the side of the white-painted cottage and pushed open the stable-style door. The top half had a polished horse cleverly fashioned as a knocker. Warm air met her as she stepped into the flagstoned kitchen. Over the fireplace, red, blue and yellow rosettes fought for room among pictures of Ali Carmichael riding Quince, her talented dappled grey mare. Malory wondered if she'd have the chance to build up a matching collection of ribbons with Tybalt.

On the scrubbed kitchen tabletop was a pile of headcollars divided into three piles according to size: pony, cob and horse. Malory took a red one from the cob pile since the bigger size would swamp Tybalt's finely shaped head. She took it out of its plastic wrapper and looked around for the waste-paper bin. She finally spotted it in a corner of the room alongside a comfy-looking chair which had a saddle draped over one of its arms. *I'd love a place like this when I'm older. Living and breathing horses even when I'm indoors!*

Tucking the new headcollar under her arm, Malory slipped out of the kitchen and closed the door behind her so none of the warmth would be lost. She retraced her footsteps to the front garden and was surprised to see a familiar car pulling up outside the picket fence. A tall dark-haired man got out of the driver's side, and as he straightened up his features were lit by the lamppost outside the gate.

Dad?

Malory stared through the dusk at her father, who was holding a bunch of cream and red flowers in one hand and trying to open the garden gate with the other. "Dad?"

Carl O'Neil looked up and Malory could have sworn a look of dismay chased across his face before he smiled. "Hey, what are you doing here?"

"I go to school here, remember?" Malory told him. She frowned, trying to remember if her dad had said he was going to drop by. *And why's he parked here?* "Was the yard's car park full?"

Mr O'Neil glanced over his shoulder. "Huh? Um, no."

"Are you here to see Ms Carmichael?" Malory stared at the bouquet of flowers. *Why's Dad brought her flowers?*

"Um." Her father's face flooded with colour as Malory narrowed her eyes. *Just what was going on here?*

"Carl!" Ms Carmichael's voice called and a moment later she appeared on the path that led to the yard. "You're early!"

Malory's stomach twisted as her riding instructor hurried up and opened her arms as if she was about to hug Carl O'Neil. She stopped abruptly when Malory's dad glanced in her direction, and her cheeks flushed deep red.

Malory found her voice. "What's going on?" She felt frozen inside. Her dad and Ms Carmichael?

No. Way.

She tried to catch her dad's eye but he wouldn't meet her gaze.

"Uh, I just remembered that I've forgotten something from my office," Ms Carmichael said, sounding as if she was being strangled. "I'll just run back and get it. Why don't you two go indoors while I'm gone?"

"And make ourselves at home?" Malory said bitterly.

Carl O'Neil placed his hand on Ali Carmichael's arm. "There's no need for you to disappear, Al."

Malory's mouth dried as Ali Carmichael pushed her hand through her hair and stepped away. "I think the two of you need some space," she said, a note of apology in her voice as she looked over at Malory.

"Some space is right," Malory said through clenched teeth. "My own." All she wanted to do was to run away as fast as she could, but that meant getting past the two people she wanted to run from.

Her breathing was ragged as she stared at her father, willing him to say something to put right her world that had just been turned upside down.

"Ali and I have been seeing each other," Mr O'Neil said in a rush. "I'd hoped you'd be pleased about it."

"When you finally got around to telling me," Malory said pointedly.

Her dad sighed. "I didn't tell you to begin with because there was no point getting you involved if it hadn't worked out."

Malory's fingernails dug into her palms. "So it's working out then." Her voice was flat.

"I thought you would be happy for me." Her father looked puzzled.

"So all the time I was trying to set you up with Matilda you were actually seeing *her*?" Malory snapped. "And even then you didn't tell me. You made me think that the reason you didn't want to be set up with someone was because you weren't over Mom." Her throat tightened.

A horrified expression stole across Mr O'Neil's face. "I had no idea that was what you thought."

"Why? Is it really so unreasonable to think you might still be missing my *mother*?" A sob tore from Malory as she pushed past her father and Ms Carmichael and yanked open the gate before racing down the path.

"Mal!"

Her father called after her but it only made her run harder. She managed to keep her distress under control all the way to Adams. She burst through the double doors, sprinted across the foyer and pelted up the stairs, thankful that no one was around to see her. Pulling open her bedroom door, she threw herself down on her bed. "Why aren't you here, Mom?" she sobbed, hugging her pillow close to her. Tears soaked into her bedlinen. "Why did you have to leave us?"

8

"Mal?" Dylan knocked on the door. "Are you in there?"

"I don't want to talk right now." Malory's voice came out as a croak.

There was a pause before Dylan opened the door and looked into the room. "I noticed Tybalt hadn't been rubbed down so I sorted him out for you."

Malory felt stricken that she had abandoned Tybalt. She tried to thank her friend but the words wouldn't come out.

"Mal?" Dylan looked more closely at her. "Are you OK?" Crossing the room, she sat on the bed. "What's wrong?"

Malory shook her head. "I'm not ready to talk about it right now." She turned away and stared at the wall.

She felt Dylan take her hand. "It must be pretty bad if you left Tybalt," she said gently, "so I'm not leaving you to deal with whatever it is on your own. You know you can tell me anything."

Mal let out a shuddering sigh and sat up, leaning her forehead on Dylan's shoulder. "My dad's dating." The words sounded totally alien, as if she needed subtitles to understand them.

Dylan gasped. "Whoa, this is a big deal! Who's he seeing?"

"Your aunt." Malory's voice was muffled against Dylan's sweater.

"You're kidding!" Dylan pulled away and stared at her in astonishment. "He's seeing Aunt Ali?"

Malory nodded.

"Shut *up*!" Dylan's eyes widened. "That's brilliant news! Aunt Ali's been on her own for ages." She grinned. "Hey, if they end up getting married, you and I will be related."

Horror rocked Malory at the thought of her dad getting remarried. "No way!" she said vehemently.

"Thanks." Dylan's expression crumpled. "We're not the Addams family, you know."

"I didn't mean. . ." Malory shook her head. "Forget it." She wasn't in the mood to try and explain to Dylan how she felt. How could she ever understand? Her mom was still alive.

Dylan frowned. "You know, I'm trying to tune in to what you're feeling but you're making it really hard. What's so wrong with my aunt? It was only five minutes ago you were trying to hook your dad up with Matilda." There was no mistaking the hurt in her voice.

Malory pressed her fingers against her temples. "Matilda was different because . . . because I knew what was going on. It was like it was my idea, not his. And nobody was lying to me."

"Nobody's lied to you now," Dylan said defensively.

Malory shrugged. "I guess that depends on whether you think hiding the truth is the same as lying."

"If Aunt Ali and your dad didn't tell us they were dating, it would have been for a good reason," Dylan said. "All that matters is that they're happy, right?"

Malory stared at her friend, seeing genuine confusion all over her face. *She just doesn't get it. She doesn't understand how I thought Dad was happy just having me to himself. I really thought he wasn't ready to move on from Mom.* And deep down, she knew it had made her feel extra close to him, and special. *You and me against the rest of the world, Dad!*

But it wasn't like that at all. He'd just been making excuses so he could chase after her *riding instructor*.

Dylan must have picked up on something of what Malory was thinking. "Just because your dad has started dating, it doesn't mean he's forgetting your mom," she said gently, "or that you are any less important to him."

Malory felt a rush of anger. "Like I said, I'm not ready to talk about this."

Sighing, Dylan stood up. "When you are, come find me, OK?"

Malory turned away and maintained a stony silence right up until Dylan closed the door. Then she curled back up on the bed and began to cry.

The next morning Malory splashed cold water over her eyes before going down to breakfast. She was last to sit down at the table and seeing her friends' anxious glances, it was clear Dylan had told them what was going on. *Oh great, now I'm the hot topic for gossip all over the school.*

"Are you OK?" Honey cleared a space for Malory's tray.

"Not really." Malory decided to be honest. Not wanting to meet Dylan's gaze, she looked down and began to toy with her granola.

"Dyl's told us what's happened." Lani broke the silence. "And I'm with her on this one. I think it's great for your dad that he's dating."

"I don't think Mal doubts whether it's good for her dad," Honey pointed out. "It's the fact that she didn't know what was going on that is so hard. She needs to have time to adjust to what's going on."

Malory looked up and snapped her fingers. "I am here, you know."

"Sorry." Honey looked startled. "I was just trying to put myself in your place."

"How about we drop this until Mal's ready?" Dylan suggested.

Ready to see things from your point of view, Malory thought as she looked down at her granola. As she pushed her spoon from one side of her bowl to the other, she couldn't help brooding on what Honey had said. *None of them can put themselves in my place*, she thought miserably. *It's not like they've lost a mother.* She considered phoning Caleb to share with him what had happened but rejected the idea almost immediately.

What if he also thought her father and Ali Carmichael getting together was a good thing?

"So, Lani, how's the science project going?" Dylan asked in a clear bid to change the topic.

"Good, thanks," Lani replied enthusiastically. "We're at the research stage of the hypothesis and we think that maybe as early as next week we'll be able to start drawing conclusions."

Malory tuned out of her friends' conversation and wondered if she ought to put in a call to her father before classes began. He'd rung the previous night but she'd refused to go down to speak to him. *And I'm still not ready*, she thought, making her mind up to phone that evening instead. *Talk about major irony. I always take all of my problems to Dad and now I've got this huge issue I need help with and I can't go to him because he's the one causing it.*

Pushing her chair back, she looked at the others. "I don't feel like any cereal. I'm going to grab some fruit instead and head over to the pool." They had swimming class first thing.

"We'll see you over there," Honey replied.

Malory nodded before turning away from the table. Usually, she thought as she made her way across campus, she'd be really looking forward to today, with a double period of swimming in the morning followed by Art and a riding lesson after lunch, but she couldn't manage to raise any enthusiasm for the day ahead. Her argument with her dad, and the way she felt about him dating Ali Carmichael, hung over her like a storm cloud.

Malory sighed and kicked out at a small pebble on the path. She watched it skitter across the bank which led down to the lake. Her stomach twisted as she thought of the times she'd sat at the water's edge and chatted with her dad, content in the knowledge that they were everything to each other. They never argued like other girls and their parents; she always figured they got on too well for that.

And now it's happening. Our first major row and all because of Ms Carmichael. Dad's never kept anything from me before and the moment she comes along he starts getting secretive.

Malory hugged her arms around herself. She'd never get used to her father dating Ali Carmichael. Never.

As soon as Malory had eaten her lunch she hurried down to the barn to spend some time with Tybalt before the lesson began. Crossing the yard, she saw Lynsey entering the barn's double doors with a knitted red hat pulled down over her long blonde hair. Malory followed her in and felt instantly soothed by the warm air with its familiar sweet smell of hay. Lynsey had gone into Blue's stall and Malory stopped by to see how the gelding was.

"He keeps squashing his bed down. He can't be comfortable lying on it." Lynsey pointed to the flattened pile of straw in the centre of the stall. "Why isn't one of the stablehands forking it over?"

"They will, but they can't be with him 24/7," Malory pointed out. "How is he today?"

"I'm sure he's worse than yesterday." Lynsey frowned.

"I think he's getting depressed." She gently stroked Blue's aristocratic grey-black nose.

"He's probably feeling fed up," Malory sympathized.

"Can you blame him?" Lynsey snapped, turning around to glare at her. "First of all he's injured through negligence on the yard and now he's stuck in his box, in pain, and probably left on his own for hours at a time when I'm in class."

He'll be getting great care, were the words on the tip of Malory's tongue, but they were silenced by a little voice whispering in her head: *Ms Carmichael was probably too wrapped up with Dad to do her job properly.*

"Maybe you should find out how often he's being checked on," she suggested instead.

"Don't worry, I will," Lynsey said grimly. She pulled open the stall door. "I'm going to get him more straw."

Malory knew she should try to calm Lynsey down. She wasn't doing herself any favours stressing over Bluegrass when she should be putting time and effort into building her relationship with Quest. But as Lynsey walked away, Malory couldn't raise the effort to call after her. "See you soon, Blue," she murmured to the roan before heading up the aisle to Tybalt.

The gelding was looking over his door and the moment he saw Malory he let out a low welcoming whicker. Malory stepped into the stall and slipped her arms around Tybalt's warm neck. "I'm so glad you're here," she sighed. "You're always the same, aren't you? You'd never lie to me."

She stayed for a while breathing in Tybalt's

comforting scent before going to fetch a grooming kit. "Since we're supposed to be looking perfect when we're jumping, how about we kick things off by making you look even more gorgeous than usual?" she suggested to the dark brown horse. Tybalt responded by flaring his nostrils and tossing his forelock.

Malory began by unbuckling the stable rug straps across Tybalt's chest. After she had peeled off his blanket, she got to work with a body brush. As his mahogany-coloured coat bloomed with a fine sheen under the brushstrokes, her thoughts turned back to her dad. She remembered how he'd known about Bluegrass' injury the day it had happened, and realized that Ali must have told him. Her throat tightened. That would have been an obvious chance for her dad to tell her that he and Ali were seeing each other. But instead he'd let her think how supportive and interested he was in her riding because he knew about the horses on the yard. *If I hadn't caught him at the cottage, how long would he have taken to tell me what was going on?*

Malory shook her head. She'd thought she and her father had been so close that they shared everything. *How wrong can a girl be?*

"In Hunt Seat Equitation, you're marked on your position, the effectiveness of your aids, and how well you maintain an even forward pace. If the judges can't choose between the best riders, they might ask for them to carry out extra movements," Ali Carmichael explained as the class cantered around the arena. "They might also throw in some questions on general horse care, so make sure you're prepared! We're going to work today on some of the movements you might get asked to do."

Dividing the class into two groups, she waved Malory's group to the lower end of the arena. "Everyone form a line," she instructed.

Malory turned Tybalt to face Ms Carmichael and halted. While she was waiting for the rest of the group to line up, she stared at her riding instructor. She was quite pretty, she admitted grudgingly. With her high cheekbones and slim figure, Malory could understand why her dad would be attracted to her. *But she's not in Mom's league.* Malory thought of her mother's laughing green eyes and raven black hair and felt a pang of longing.

Ms Carmichael ended Malory's scrutiny by calling her attention back to the class. "I'd like you all to ride four steps of rein back," she announced. "I'm looking for your horses to move straight with feet clearly raised and set down almost simultaneously in diagonal pairs. No shuffling, please! You might want to ride forward first and achieve a balanced halt before asking for the rein back."

Malory's heart sank. Tybalt hated reining back, and Malory suspected it was because he couldn't see the point of it. If he wanted to get somewhere, he'd turn round and go forwards! Squeezing her legs against his warm flanks, she waited to feel for Tybalt to reach forward. The moment the gelding's weight shifted, she closed her hands on the reins while keeping up the pressure behind the girth. Tybalt threw up his head and flattened his ears. Beside her, Lynsey got Quest to take two steps back before riding him forward again.

"That's OK, Lynsey, at least the steps he took were nicely formed," Ms Carmichael commented before turning her attention to Malory. "Walk forward, halt, and try again."

"He hates doing this," Malory argued. "It's just going to get him wound up and in a bad mood for the rest of the lesson."

"All the more reason for getting him to accept the movement," Ms Carmichael told her. "When you're competing in an equitation class, telling the judge that Tybalt hates rein back isn't going to get you any marks."

Malory clamped her lips into a thin line and prepared to give the commands for the second time. Tybalt swished his tail and swung his quarters out.

"Come on, Malory. It's not up to Tybalt to decide what he does in a lesson," Ali Carmichael reminded her. "Keep trying." She walked on to Lucy, who was next in line.

Malory stared angrily at her instructor's back before closing her legs on Tybalt. "Come on, Tyb, just a couple of steps." Knowing that the rest of the class was waiting for her and Tybalt made Malory flustered. Tybalt snorted and tossed his head. Resisting the temptation to try to haul him back with the reins, Malory kept up a gentle pressure and willed Tybalt to co-operate. The gelding took two hurried steps back before swinging out his quarters and raising his head to fight the pressure on the bit.

Ali Carmichael walked over. "Let's get him to rein back off a turn on the forehand," she suggested. "That way he'll be in a more comfortable position to carry out the movement. Ride a quarter turn and then go straight into rein back."

With her cheeks flaming at being singled out, Malory rode Tybalt out of the line-up. She halted and used her inside leg to hold his forehand in place while using her outside leg behind the girth to push his hindquarters around. When she felt Tybalt's back round, Malory asked him to take a step backward. Smoothly Tybalt took one step, then another.

"Good," Ms Carmichael called. "Walk him forward as a reward."

Malory patted Tybalt's sweat-slick neck and released the rein contact while squeezing with her legs. He walked forward eagerly with his ears pricked.

"You're going to have to get him happy with the rein back before the All Schools League competition," Ali Carmichael told her. "We've got five days to go and we can't afford to lose precious marks. OK, class, swap ends."

Malory stared down at Tybalt's mane until it blurred. *She just picked the worst exercise possible for Tybalt and me to do, and humiliated us in front of everyone else. Is this her way of getting back at me?*

She trotted to the top of the arena while the other

half of the class rode down to Ms Carmichael. Dylan halted Morello alongside her. "Are you OK?"

"Fine," Malory said shortly.

"Lynsey and Quest seem a bit happier today," Dylan commented, watching them circle their riding instructor.

Malory looked down the arena to where Lynsey was smoothly rising to the trot on the dappled grey. Although they looked more at ease, they were still nowhere near the harmony level Lynsey had with Bluegrass.

Honey rode up on Minnie, who had reined back in a straight line as if she walked backwards all the time. "Are you all right, Mal?"

"What is it with everyone? Tybalt and I have a problem with one movement and it's like the whole class turns into the equitation police," Malory said in exasperation.

Honey coloured and bit her lower lip before turning Minnie away.

"That was way harsh," Dylan said quietly. "Why don't you chill out a bit?"

Malory glared at her friend. *Chill?* Didn't she understand how impossible that was? The only way she'd relax right now was being told that thinking Ali Carmichael and her dad were dating had been one huge misunderstanding.

"I'm sorry, boy. I guess I let you down today," Malory said as she unbuckled Tybalt's throatlash.

Tybalt gave a long sigh before rubbing his cheek

against her arm. Slipping his bridle off, Malory hung it up before going to undo his saddle.

"So what happened back there?" Ali Carmichael asked as she stepped into the stall.

Malory froze, her hand on the girth buckles. "What do you mean?"

"I mean that I haven't seen Tybalt that uptight in aeons." Ms Carmichael frowned. "I hope you're not letting any personal issues interfere with your riding, Malory. Anything that affects your focus needs to be left outside the arena."

Malory slowly undid each buckle, willing the riding instructor to leave.

"You owe that much to Tybalt," Ali Carmichael went on. She turned to leave before glancing back. "Come up to the house any time you're ready to talk things through, OK?"

Malory became ultra-absorbed in lowering the girth under Tybalt's stomach and when she finally looked up she saw that Ms Carmichael had gone. *I don't want to talk things through*, she thought in frustration. *I want to pretend they never happened.*

That night Malory made her way down to the foyer to call her dad. She hesitated as she picked up the receiver. How should she play this? Should she be apologetic? *No way*, she thought. *I'm not the one who's been sneaking around and telling lies.* Feeling nervous, she tapped in her home number. "Hi," she said when her father answered.

"Hey there, sweetheart. I'm really glad you called. If

I hadn't gotten to speak to you tonight I'd have driven up."

"To see me or your girlfriend?" Malory couldn't resist saying.

"Mal, you'll always be number one in my life. Just because I'm dating Ms Carmichael, it doesn't mean anything between you and I has changed," he said softly.

"Apart from not being a hundred-per-cent honest with each other any more," she corrected.

"It was wrong of me not to tell you I had gone out with Ali a few times." Her dad sighed. "But I need you to understand that it was only because I didn't want to get you emotionally involved until I knew it was something worth being emotionally involved in."

Malory's heart began to pound. "And is it?"

"I think so," he told her. "And we'd very much like you to be OK with it."

We. Malory's fingers tightened against the phone. "It's all a bit much for me to take in right now," she said hoarsely.

"OK," Carl O'Neil conceded. "I'd rather do this face to face than over the phone anyway. We'll talk properly on Saturday after the competition."

"I don't want you to be there." As the words came out of her mouth, Malory realized that she didn't mean it. She wanted her dad to prove how much he really loved her. *Say that you'll come anyway*, she begged silently.

"You know how much I want to be there," Mr O'Neil said. "But I'm not going to do anything to upset you on your big day." His voice was heavy. "If that's really what you want, then I won't come."

Tears blurred Malory's vision as she said goodbye and hung up the phone. *No*, she thought helplessly, *it isn't what I want at all. None of this is.*

9

"Mal, you need to wake up." Alexandra's voice woke Malory out of a deep sleep.

Malory struggled to focus her thoughts. Was she late for registration? Did she have double Maths first thing? Suddenly she realized that it wasn't a school day but Saturday.

"The competition!" she gasped. "I was supposed to get up at six. How late am I?"

"You're OK," Alexandra reassured her. "You might have slept through your alarm but I didn't!"

Malory swung her legs off the bed. "You're a life saver!" Checking the display on her alarm, she was relieved to see that it was two minutes past six.

"This is one of the reasons why I don't do horses." Alexandra yawned as she climbed back into bed and snuggled under her duvet.

"It's not all early mornings!" Malory yawned, too, as she reached for her jeans and sweater. Her show clothes were hanging on the outside of her wardrobe above her boots which she'd polished to a shine the previous night. She was determined that she and Tybalt were going to look their absolute best for the equitation competition. *I just wish Dad was going to be here to see us.* Pushing away that unhelpful thought, she grabbed the muffin she'd brought up from the canteen the night before. As she headed down to the yard she pulled off the wrapper and made herself eat despite the butterflies fluttering in her stomach.

The barn doors were open, spilling light on to the yard. In the first stall Quest, who had been moved alongside Bluegrass, looked out. Malory paused to stroke his nose. "Hey, boy, are you all set for today?"

"He'd better be." Lynsey came up behind her and placed a saddle on the half wall.

Malory watched her open the stall door. "Last night's practice went OK," she reminded her. They had jumped a course of jumps and practised different equitation movements. Apart from one knock-down, Lynsey and Quest had gone clear, even if it hadn't been with the same perfect unity that she was used to with Bluegrass.

Lynsey raised her eyebrows. "I take it you're not talking about you and Tybalt?" Tybalt had taken three hurried steps back before refusing point blank to do any more.

Malory groaned. "Cut me some slack."

"I think that's what Tybalt was asking for." Lynsey offered a weak smile.

Malory's eyebrows shot up. Could it be that she and Lynsey were actually bantering? "Who knows what goes on in Tybalt's head?" she said ruefully.

Lynsey sighed. "I wish we could read their minds. It would make things so much easier."

"If Amy Fleming was here, she'd tell you that even if you can't read their minds, you can pick up some pretty strong clues about their personalities," Malory said, raising her voice as Kelly walked past pushing a wheelbarrow.

Lynsey looked cynical as she picked up a body brush from her grooming kit. "Amy's that veterinary student who came here to give a symposium, right? The one who's into all of that alternative stuff?"

Malory nodded. "She came to help me with Tybalt when he first arrived here." She tensed, waiting for the inevitable sarcastic response about Tybalt's early problems.

"So what do you think she'd say about Quest?" was all Lynsey said as she began brushing through the grey's mane.

Malory thought back to one particular article by Amy in which she'd analysed equine facial features. Then she looked closely at the big dappled gelding. "Quest's eyes are large and round, and that shows an honest and reliable temperament," she explained. "Because they're set well apart, he'll be smart and a fast learner, which means he'll adjust to you a lot more quickly than you're adjusting to him." She glanced at Lynsey, who had stopped brushing Quest. "Not that I'm implying you're not smart!" she added hastily.

"Keep going," Lynsey said, her expression inscrutable as she stood back and stared at Quest.

Malory looked at Quest's nostrils and mouth as he nosed hopefully at his empty bucket. "He's got a long mouth which makes him highly sensitive, which I guess means he's going to be like a Geiger counter to your mood." She frowned. "I can't remember any more, sorry."

"So basically he's going to turn in a good performance for me as long as I treat him as super-sensitive, super-intelligent and super-reliable," Lynsey murmured.

"I guess that about sums it up," Malory agreed with a half-smile.

Lynsey pursed her lips and looked thoughtful. "It's not been easy adjusting to a new horse. I've been riding Blue for two years."

"And it must have been tough concentrating on Quest when you were worrying about Bluegrass," Malory said sympathetically.

Lynsey nodded. "Do you think it's too late to make a breakthrough with Quest? We haven't exactly made for a red rosette combination so far."

Malory hesitated. "He's got a kind personality which I guess should make him open to forming a last-minute partnership. You've had more riding instruction than the rest of us put together, and those skills are going to work just as well on Quest as they do on Blue. I'm sure Quest will try his heart out for you if you give him the chance." An idea suddenly occurred to her. "Something that Amy showed me was how to massage lavender oil into Tybalt to help him relax, but it also helped us to bond. How about I give you some for Quest?"

For a moment she thought Lynsey was going to refuse. Then she shrugged, swinging her blonde ponytail over her shoulder. "That would be good. Thanks, Mal," she said after a pause.

As Malory turned to go and fetch the bottle of oil, she heard Lynsey say in a low voice, "I guess you're not doing such a bad job as captain after all."

Malory looked back in surprise but Lynsey's attention was back on Quest while she stroked the gelding's nose. *What a shock*, Malory thought as she headed to the tack room. *But for once, it's a nice shock!*

Malory carefully rolled up the last of Tybalt's plaits and inserted her sewing needle.

"Wow, Tybalt looks amazing!" Lani walked into the stall dressed in white jodhpurs and a spotless black jacket with high boots. "Honey and I are just about to go walk the course before warming up," she told her. Lani and Honey's open class was scheduled ahead of the team classes. The equitation was divided into two phases, the first that morning was over fences whilst the afternoon was on the flat. The marks would be added up and the winners announced after the last class.

"OK. I'm about to go get changed too," Malory said as she snipped off the thread. "I'll come and warm up with you as soon as I'm done."

Lani lifted Tybalt's stable rug off the wall and helped Malory slip it over him. "Dylan's already gone to get into her show clothes," she said over a clatter of hooves as Abigail led Hardy out of the opposite stall.

Malory felt a little surprised. Usually they would have walked back to Adams together. *But she's already made it clear whose side she's on at the moment, and it's not mine.*

"OK, I'm out of here. Wish me luck," Lani said as she left the stall.

"Good luck," Malory called after her. Patting Tybalt on his shoulder, she stepped into the aisle and waited for Alice Sykes to lead Falcon by.

Out on the yard, riders were preparing to ride down to the outdoor arena to warm up. Glancing at her watch, Malory realized that there was just over an hour before her first class began. She hurried up to her room and put on the clothes she'd left out that morning, leaving her black gloves until last. With a quick glance in the mirror to check that her tie was pinned tidily, she went back down to the barn.

Kelly was carrying two saddles out of the tack room. "Tybalt's tack's over his wall," she told Malory. "And Ms Carmichael's asked me to remind you and the rest of the team to meet her in the arena before your class begins so she can walk you around the course."

"OK, thanks," Malory said, hurrying down the aisle. Tybalt looked at her expectantly, his dark eyes glowing. "You know it's a competition day, don't you?" Malory said, dropping a kiss on his nose. She peeled back his rug before tacking him up. "Everything we do today has to be perfect," she told him as she led him out of his stall.

Once she was mounted, Malory followed the track down to the outdoor arena which was full of competitors warming up, not just from Chestnut Hill but from the other schools that took part in the League. A familiar grey horse was cantering towards the practice fence which had been set up in the middle of the arena. Recognizing Caleb on his striking gelding, Gent, Malory halted Tybalt at the edge of the ring. She watched, impressed, as Gent sailed over the pole in a businesslike fashion. With a flick of his tail, he landed clear and cantered away. Malory had exchanged a few emails with Caleb since the start of term, but she hadn't had a chance to speak to him yet. They'd both been busy with preparations for the competition – and when Caleb had suggested meeting up in Cheney Falls last week, Malory had been preoccupied with setting up her dad and Matilda Harvey. She winced as she thought about how excited she'd been.

Caleb knew nothing about Operation Lunchdate, nor what had happened since. Now wasn't the time to tell him, but Malory knew she'd struggle to hide how worried she was. She debated whether to ride down to the lower field which was also being used as a warm-up area, but decided she'd rather put up with the risk of dealing with some probing questions from Caleb than jarring Tybalt's joints on the hard ground in the other arena. She could always promise to talk to him later.

In fact, the schooling ring was so crowded that Caleb only had a chance to wave at Malory from the other side before he was hidden behind a serious-looking girl on a long-backed chestnut mare. As Malory steered Tybalt through the open gate, she saw Dylan, Honey and Lani trotting a circle in the lower corner of the arena. Riding towards them, she saw Mr and Mrs Harper and Sam looking over the rails.

"You're all looking fantastic!" Mrs Harper called in her cute English accent. "I'm sure you're going to shoot the Chestnut Hill score sky high today."

Honey patted Minnie's proudly arched neck. The mare was stepping out with an exaggerated high movement and her silver tail was kinked over her back. "I wish it were just down to looks!" Honey sighed.

Her brother Sam grinned. "I'm not so sure. Those riding helmets aren't the most flattering headgear, you know!"

"Ah yes, you're a brave man with the insults when there's a fence between us!" Lani brandished her whip jokingly towards him.

"We're going to go get some seats in the arena," Mr Harper said, cupping his hand over Sam's mouth to stop any more smart remarks. "We just wanted to wish you luck."

As she watched them walk away, Malory felt a stab of sadness that she didn't have anyone here supporting her. She wished like crazy that she hadn't told her dad not to come. It would have been great to have him here wishing her luck and knowing he was rooting for her while she competed. *And he would have been if it wasn't for Ali Carmichael*, she thought angrily. Tybalt snorted and threw up his head.

"Sorry, Tyb," Malory said, relaxing her hold on the reins. She had to remember how sensitive Tybalt was;

he was even better than Honey at knowing when something was wrong!

Over the loudspeaker came the announcement for the Open Jumping and Equitation Class. Honey and Lani turned Colorado and Minnie to ride out of the arena.

"Go, Honey! Go, Lani!" Dylan called.

"Good luck," Malory added. She watched them trot away before facing Tybalt at the practice jump. She felt herself start to relax as Tybalt cantered tidily towards the rail and rose effortlessly into the air.

Caleb trotted away from the knot of riders on the outside track and rode alongside her. "Tybalt's looking good."

"Thanks." Malory felt a rush of pride as she patted Tybalt's neck.

"Are you OK? It feels like I haven't seen you in ages." Caleb turned Gent in step with Tybalt as they rode down the arena.

Malory glanced at him. Christmas suddenly seemed like aeons ago. "It has been a long time," she agreed.

"So everything's been OK?" Caleb prompted.

Malory hesitated. Now wasn't the time to say, *My dad's been seeing Ms Carmichael and I've only just found out about it*. She forced a smile. "Everything's fine," she replied.

"Good." Caleb half halted Gent. "We'll catch up properly later. Good luck for today."

"You too." Malory pushed away the niggling feeling of guilt that she wasn't being totally honest. *Like father, like daughter*, a voice whispered in her head. A palomino pony cantered past close by and Tybalt skittered away from it, swinging his quarters out and nearly crashing into a big black mare who had come up on the other side.

Malory scooped up her reins and apologized breathlessly to the girl on the mare. "That's enough nonsense. From now until the end of the competition, I'm just going to concentrate on you and me," she told Tybalt. *There'll be plenty of time to think about Dad and Ali later.*

After the Open Class, there was a short interval while the jumps were altered for the start of the team jumping. Malory tied Tybalt outside the barn and went to walk the course with Ali Carmichael and the rest of the team. The first thing she noticed was how many turns they'd have to negotiate between the fences. Beside her, Dylan groaned.

Malory glanced at her friend. It was time to be team captain, and not think about their recent quarrel. "Just think one turn at a time," she advised. "And don't forget that in our last few practice sessions, you and Morello have totally nailed jumping out of corners."

Dylan nodded distractedly as she paced the distance between the first and second fence.

"That's good advice," Ali Carmichael agreed.

Malory stared at her instructor for a moment and then went to join the others in pacing out how many strides Tybalt would have to put in between the upright and parallel.

After they had walked the course, Ali Carmichael took them back to one particularly sharp turn. As they retraced the line they'd have to take, she warned, "If you cut the corner you'll arrive at the fence half a stride too short, and if you let your horse drift out you're going to be half a stride too long. The temptation when you're riding against the clock is literally to cut corners, but you can't afford to lose control on the turns. Anything to add, Mal?"

Malory shrugged. "I don't think my opinion really matters."

Beside her, Dylan took in a sharp breath.

Malory's cheeks burned as she realized just how rude she'd sounded. *But it's too late now.* She was determined that she wasn't going to be the one to back down.

"As team captain, your opinion counts very much," Ali Carmichael said quietly, "but if you think that I've covered everything then you can all go and get mounted up. Good luck, everyone, and don't forget you're picking up marks for equitation. You're going to be judged on the harmony you have with your horse and the control you show. The judges will also be awarding marks for your position and how effectively and consistently you ride."

Malory was aware of Lucy and Joanna giving her curious looks as they walked back out of the arena behind the team from Wycliffe College. Only Lynsey hadn't seemed to notice the tension between the team captain and their riding instructor. Noticing that Lynsey was gnawing her lower lip, Malory realized she was probably too caught up with some highly unfamiliar nerves to pay attention to anything else.

As they went to untie the horses outside the barn, Malory looked around for Dylan to wish her good luck. But Dylan had ducked behind Morello and was fiddling with his girths as if she was deliberately avoiding Malory. It kind of made sense that she was offended on behalf of her aunt – Mal knew she'd been out of line. *Why can't Dylan see how difficult this is for me?*

Holding back a sigh, she went to talk to Joanna and Lucy. "Skylark can turn on a dime so this course is perfect for him," she told Lucy, "and consistency is Calvin's middle name but keep your legs on to remind him that we need speed as well as steadiness." The girls nodded, and Malory noticed that Lucy looked a little pale. "You'll be great." She squeezed her arm reassuringly.

Above their heads, the loudspeaker crackled into life: *First to ride for the junior team hunt seat equitation class is Joanna Boardman for Chestnut Hill on Calvin.*

"You're on," Malory said to Joanna. "Good luck!"

As Joanna trotted towards the arena entrance, Malory navigated a path through the crowded yard to untie Tybalt. She checked her girth before reaching up to slip off his headcollar. "We need to put in the performance of our lives today," she murmured, remembering how nervous Lynsey had looked earlier. It was the first time Malory had faced up to the fact that she might have to make up marks that Lynsey lost. "Do you think you can do that for me?" she asked the dark brown gelding.

Tybalt brushed his muzzle over her cheek as if he was giving her a kiss. Malory stroked his nose as the loudspeaker announced: *Joanna Boardman for Chestnut Hill, six faults. Next to ride, Lynsey Harrison on Knight's Quest, also for Chestnut Hill.*

"I'll be back in a minute," Malory promised Tybalt as she hurried back across the yard. She squeezed through the people crowded around the entrance and watched as Lynsey cantered a circle. They made a showy combination, with Lynsey in her white jodhpurs, gleaming black boots and bespoke black coat. Quest had been groomed to perfection and looked nicely collected as he headed towards the first fence. Neatly folding his front legs, his jump looked effortless as he cleared the upright. Lynsey sat still as they cantered towards the parallel bars and Quest took off at just the right place. With a small snort, he put on a spurt of speed to clear the hurdle and as they turned towards the gate Lynsey stayed upright and deep in the saddle, keeping Quest in a correct outline while encouraging him to put in enough impulsion to clear the top rail.

They're going great! Malory felt a rush of admiration for the way Lynsey had put her worries about Blue to one side to put in a professional performance on Quest. With his generous nature, he was responding to her sympathetic riding by putting in a hundred-per-cent effort. As they went clear fence after fence, Malory's hopes soared. They approached the final jump, a triple pole, in a smooth rhythmic canter. Quest pricked his ears forward and cleared it with inches to spare.

Applause echoed around the arena as Lynsey leaned forward to pat Quest's neck.

Lynsey Harrison, on Knight's Quest for Chestnut Hill, goes clear in one minute fifty-five. Next to ride is Joseph Arnold on Rocky Horror for Saint Christopher's.

Malory waited for Lynsey to trot out of the arena. "That was fantastic!" she exclaimed.

Lynsey looked flushed. "He was, wasn't he?" she agreed. "He hasn't got Blue's polish but he did well."

Malory patted Quest before heading back to Tybalt. "You've got quite an act to follow," she told him as she swung up in the saddle, "but I know how brilliant you can be. Just don't prove me wrong!" She decided to give him five minutes in the outdoor arena before going to the collecting yard.

The arena was beginning to fill with senior riders warming up but Malory found a quiet spot where she could concentrate on getting Tybalt to bring his quarters underneath him and lighten his forehand. She lost track of time and was startled by her name being called over the loudspeaker: *Next we have Malory O'Neil on Tybalt for Chestnut Hill.*

Her mouth dry with nerves, Malory trotted through the open gateway and up the path to the yard.

"Good luck!" Caleb called from where he was standing near the entrance.

Malory gave him a brief smile before riding into the arena. Immediately opposite, on the far side, she could see Ms Carmichael sitting behind the judges' box. Malory suddenly felt filled with a determination to prove just what she and Tybalt could achieve. Trying to blank out the sea of faces in the viewing gallery, she squeezed Tybalt into a canter. As the electric buzzer sounded, she turned Tybalt to the first fence.

"Now, Tyb," she murmured, closing her legs around him. Tybalt responded by rising into the air and sailing over the coloured poles. Once they had landed, Malory concentrated on keeping Tybalt's forward momentum by closing her legs on the girth while controlling his speed with her hands. As his hooves thudded clear after the second fence, Malory fixed her gaze on the tricky hurdle that came next. She kept Tybalt heading down the line she had walked before, so that he approached it slightly on the left. He popped over the rail easily, and Malory sat deep to turn him on the left rein towards the gate. Potted plants, some with bright red flowers, had been placed on either side of the fence and Malory kept up a reassuring contact as she felt Tybalt hesitate.

"Come on, Tyb, you can do this," she told him.

Tybalt put in an extra high leap that lifted him several inches above the gate, and the moment they landed Malory shifted her weight in the saddle for the next turn. She kept her inside leg on and controlled Tybalt's hindquarters with her outside leg so that they cantered steadily around the corner. The moment they were on the straight Malory urged Tybalt forward. The red-painted wall loomed in front of them but Tybalt met the challenge with a flick of his tail, and Malory felt a surge of exhilaration as he flew over the blocks. Cantering across the diagonal, they dealt with the oxer followed by the parallel, and then tackled the upright in the corner of the arena. Malory sat deep on the sharp turn and used her legs strongly to stop Tybalt from drifting as they quickened their pace for the water jump.

She caught a glimpse of the ticking clock above the judges' box and realized they needed to keep the pace on if they were going to avoid time faults. She closed her legs and encouraged Tybalt to lengthen his stride as they raced towards the next fence, a red and white upright. They only had one more fence to make it a clear round. Turning towards the triple pole, Malory half halted Tybalt before squeezing with her legs to bring the gelding's hindlegs right underneath him. With a surge of power, Tybalt launched himself into the air. Malory's heart soared as she heard thunderous applause. They'd gone clear!

That was a clear round for Malory O'Neil on Tybalt for Chestnut Hill in one minute fifty-two, said the announcer.

Malory leaned forward and patted Tybalt's neck. "Good boy!" she gasped. "You were amazing!"

But her sense of triumph was dampened by the thought that her dad hadn't been there to see her. Malory suddenly wished with all her heart that he had been. He might not need her in his life any more – but she still needed him.

10

"Brilliant job, Mal!" Caleb held up his hand to give her a high five before turning to rub Tybalt's nose. "And you. You're turning into the secret weapon of Team CH."

"What do you mean, turning into? He's always been our secret weapon!" Malory pretended to be indignant before breaking into a smile. Slipping down from the saddle, she ducked under the flap to loosen her girth.

Caleb followed her over to the barn where Gent was tied. "Tybalt's getting better every time I see him," he commented.

Malory felt a rush of pride. "Thanks. He's pretty amazing, that's for sure." She turned and looked up at the handsome ninth-grader. "I guess I should wish you good luck, even if you are the opposition," she said mischievously.

Caleb grinned. "Only when I'm riding. Catch you later."

"Later," Malory echoed. After Caleb had trotted away on the big grey gelding, she led Tybalt around the yard to cool off. She was surprised not to see any sign of her friends. She pushed away a feeling of disappointment, reminding herself that they had their own schedules to stick to. *I guess Honey and Lani will be in the barn and Dylan will be somewhere warming Morello up.* "Come on, Tyb," she said after ten minutes. "Let's get you back to your stall."

Kelly greeted Malory as she led Tybalt up the central aisle. "How did you go?" She paused collecting the contents of a grooming kit outside Kingfisher's stall.

"Clear in one fifty-two," Malory told her. "Tyb was a star!"

"Sounds like you both were." Kelly smiled. "Well done, Mal."

Malory took Tybalt into his stall. "We make some team, huh?" she said, giving him a swift hug. Tybalt rubbed his head against her shoulder, almost knocking her off balance. "Is that better now?" she laughed as she reached up to slip the bridle over his hot, damp ears.

The moment he was free of his tack, Tybalt shook himself vigorously, like a dog getting out of a bath. Malory fetched a bucket and sponge and washed him down before buckling on his anti-sweat rugs. "I'll be back soon," she promised him. She rinsed his mouth out but didn't let him take a long drink, and put his hay net outside his stall, where he looked at it sadly. "Sorry, no food or water until we've finished." They were riding in their second equitation class in an hour's time.

Malory headed over to the student centre to get a chicken wrap for a hasty lunch before making her way back to the barn. Lani and Honey were mounted and waiting with the rest of the competitors for the second phase of the open equitation. Malory made her way past a group of riders from Wycliffe College to the middle of the yard where Lani and Honey were standing.

"I just wanted to wish you good luck," she told them. She smiled as Colorado nosed hopefully at her pocket. "Don't slime my best jacket!" She took a quick step back. "How did you guys get on in the jumping?"

"I don't know how many marks we'd have picked up for equitation," Lani replied, pulling a face. "I looked like a paper parcel that's coming untied, although Honey is always picture perfect."

"They're not just giving marks for how neat you look," Honey reminded her.

"Guys! How did you get on in the jumping?" Malory asked again.

"I got two faults and Lani got six," Honey told her. "There were only two clear rounds but we don't know how the judges will end up scoring. We need to go all out in this next class, whatever."

"No worries there," Malory said loyally. Flatwork was Honey's strength. She and Minnie were bound to score high.

Lani shortened her reins as Colorado tried to walk forward. "How about you?"

"I went clear," Malory replied. "So did Lynsey. I'm not sure how Dylan went. I haven't seen her yet."

"That's fantastic news!" Honey exclaimed. "Talk about sending the team's score into orbit!"

"Maybe after today we'll have pulled back on the

leader board." Lani punched the air. "Your dad must be rapt!"

Out of the corner of her eye, Malory noticed Ali Carmichael heading over. "I've got to go and get Tybalt ready," she said hastily, not wanting to admit she'd told her father not to come. "I'll catch you guys later. Good luck!"

"You too," Lani and Honey chorused.

Hurrying away, Malory skirted around the horses and riders and headed into the barn. She paused outside Morello's stall and looked over the door. Dylan was brushing the gelding's already gleaming coat.

Malory could feel the tension in the air between them but she didn't know how to ease it. Dylan was obviously mad at her for her attitude towards Ali Carmichael. *But she doesn't even want to try to see things from my point of view.* "All the best for our next class," Malory said.

"OK." Dylan ducked down to brush the feathers on Morello's legs.

Feeling annoyed at her friend's stubborn off-handedness, Malory headed down the aisle to Tybalt. At least she could rely on him not to take sides against her!

"Steady, Tyb." Malory hoped it wouldn't be much longer before the class was called into the arena. The yard was crammed with riders from each of the competing junior teams and Tybalt was getting stressed. She felt a rush of relief when over the loudspeaker came the announcement for the start of the class. Squeezing Tybalt forward, she rode up alongside Lynsey.

"Quest looks ready to dazzle all over again," she commented. The dappled grey had his ears pricked, and his eyes were bright as he looked at the horses around him.

Lynsey nodded. "He's doing a good job filling in for Blue," she said, sounding surprised. "I guess it's not his fault he's not quite in the same league," she added before they rode through the entrance.

Malory tried not to look too astounded. *Wow! High praise from Lynsey!*

The moment Tybalt's hooves hit the soft surface, she pushed every thought from her mind so she could focus on each signal she needed to give. Glancing over at the judges' box, she saw them scrutinizing each rider as they passed in front of them. *Harmony and control,* Malory told herself as the senior judge asked the class to trot. She shortened her reins and gave Tybalt a slight squeeze with her leg until he smoothly increased his stride. As they turned down the diagonal to change rein, Malory concentrated on keeping supple and relaxed in the saddle. Ahead of her, Ellen Staddon from Allbright's was tipped forward and her arms were stiff. Her bay mare was above the bit, trying to avoid contact.

"Canter, please," the judge requested, and one by one the riders sent their horses into a canter in front of the judges' box.

"Stay with me, Tyb," Malory murmured, warning him with a half halt that he wasn't to canter until she told him. Tybalt flicked back his ear at the sound of her voice and Malory could feel his eagerness to run. As they approached the judges, Malory half halted again and shifted her weight slightly inward, using her inside leg to ask for impulsion while pushing her outside leg behind the girth. *Keep straight, keep straight*, she thought in time to his rhythmic strides.

After the class had cantered twice around the arena, the judges called for a halt and made notes as each of the riders brought their horse to a stop. In the far corner of the arena, Caleb and Gent halted perfectly and stood square. Malory half halted Tybalt to make sure he was balanced and on the bit before riding him smoothly to a stop. For once Tybalt stood absolutely still, standing straight and square with his weight distributed evenly. Malory was surprised at the amount of riders who had difficulty carrying out a halt. More than a few of the class had come to a ragged stop without their horses standing square.

At the judge's signal to quit stirrups, Malory transferred her reins into one hand and crossed the irons in front of her. The class trotted and then cantered without stirrups and Malory suddenly realized she was enjoying herself. Tybalt's stride was rounded and his ears pricked forward as he carried her around the arena. Malory didn't have to see him to know that his eyes were shining. When they halted a second time, the senior judge stepped from the box. Walking into the centre of the arena, he nodded at Sienna Macleod and Gemma Ashdon from Allbright's, and Joseph and Caleb from St Kit's. He then called in Lynsey before finally looking over at Malory and inclining his head. With her heart pounding, Malory rode Tybalt into the centre of the arena alongside Lynsey and the others while the rest of the class rode out.

The senior judge ran his eyes over each of the remaining five riders. "Ride a turn on the forehand, please."

Malory's mouth went dry as she realized one of the next instructions might be to rein back. Picking up on her sudden tension, Tybalt raised his head.

"Get a grip," Lynsey whispered.

Taking a deep breath, Malory used both legs to keep the impulsion forward while using her reins to regulate the bend and stop Tybalt from stepping forward. Her inside leg guided Tybalt as he stepped smoothly around, his rhythm consistent as he completed the turn.

"And now four steps of rein back please," the senior judge requested. Malory's heart began to thud. *I'm not going to let Tybalt down*, she suddenly thought. *We're a team, and he needs to know I'm with him one hundred per cent on this*. But as she closed her legs and kept a pressure on the reins, Tybalt stiffened. Beside them, Quest calmly stepped back.

"Come on, Tyb. Pretend we're dancing," Malory murmured, and then began to hum under her breath. She knew Tyb wouldn't exactly hear the tune and start tapping his toes, but if it helped her to relax, it would make her aids a lot clearer. Sure enough, Tybalt dropped his head and slowly took one step back, followed by another.

"Clever boy," Malory whispered, feeling as if she was about to burst with pride.

One by one they were asked to canter a figure eight with flying changes. Tybalt cantered two strides on the wrong leg before Malory could get him to change lead. Settling into his rhythm, she concentrated on keeping him collected right until the very last stride.

"OK, thank you all very much." The senior judge nodded and turned back to the judges' box. Applause and cheers followed the riders out of the arena as they joined the other junior riders on the crowded yard. Malory nudged Tybalt over to where the rest of the junior team were waiting.

"You and Lynsey were both held back!" Lucy exclaimed. "That's gotta mean some serious points to our overall score."

Malory swapped an amused glance with Lynsey. "Here's hoping!"

Over the buzz of conversation the loudspeaker came into life. Everyone fell silent as they listened to the junior equitation classes' final scores.

The placings for the junior open and team equitation classes are as follows: for the open jumping, in fourth position Anna Fenton from Allbright's riding on Maddy. Malory watched Anna ride her black gelding with three white socks into the arena to fresh applause. *Third place goes to Felicity Harper on Moonlight Minuet.*

Grinning with delight, Malory half turned in her

saddle as she searched the yard for Honey. From the far corner, Honey rode Minnie forward. Her cheeks were flushed as she rode inside the arena. Nobody else from Chestnut Hill was placed but in the open flatwork class Jennifer Quinn came fourth and Honey was second!

"We'd better get decent results for the junior team classes," Lynsey muttered. "Or we're going to slip even further down the league table."

Malory looked down and fiddled with a strand of Tybalt's mane. It was impossible to know where each rider had been placed because of the extra marks awarded for equitation.

Here are the results for the junior teams' equitation: in fourth place with a total of sixty-two points, Wycliffe College.

"At least we're not bottom," Joanna said to Lynsey as the Wycliffe team rode into the arena.

"We're not third either!" Lucy said excitedly as the loudspeaker called St Kit's. As more space appeared in the yard, Dylan rode Morello over to join the rest of the team. Forgetting their earlier tension, Malory reached over to squeeze her arm.

In second position, with seventy-two points, is Allbright's and in first place, and winners of the equitation event, with seventy-four points, is Chestnut Hill!

An explosion of cheers and applause came from inside the arena. "Well done, guys, you totally deserve this," Malory told her team. She met Lynsey's eyes.

"Especially with one equine member of our team out

of the running right now." She raised her voice over the loudspeaker that was calling them in. "You can tell Blue we won the trophy in his honour!"

Lynsey held her gaze. "Thanks. That means a lot."

Dylan clutched Malory's arm. "Did you hear that?"

"What?" Malory frowned.

"The loudspeaker!" Dylan's eyes shone. "You won the individual trophy for best rider!"

Malory stared. "No way!"

"Guys, we're not going to pick up any trophies if we don't get in there," Joanna pointed out.

"I'm so psyched I'm not sure I can keep in the saddle!" Malory laughed as she squeezed Tybalt forward.

"You're going to have to, or they'll question whether they've awarded the prize to the right person." But Lynsey's putdown lacked its usual acerbic tone, and as the team rode into the centre of the arena Malory was brimming over with joy.

The senior judge came to speak to Malory as the other judges handed out the ribbons. "Well done," he congratulated her. "We were all very impressed with the communication you had with your horse."

"I thought we were going to run out when you asked for a rein back," Malory confessed.

The judge smiled. "I could see he tensed up but you handled him pitch perfect. Congratulations!"

To a storm of applause, Malory led the victory lap around the arena. But as the crowd roared their approval Malory felt a big empty space inside of her, dragging her down.

Dad should be here, she thought as they clattered out on to the yard.

Ali Carmichael had hurried around to greet the team. Her cheeks were pink as she smiled up at them, and tendrils of hair had escaped from her ponytail. "Well done, everyone. I couldn't be prouder!"

She was really nice, Malory admitted grudgingly. And if Ali Carmichael had been embarking on a romance with any other guy Malory would have thought him lucky. *But it's not just any other guy, it's my dad.*

"And gaining the individual trophy is a massive compliment to your riding. You did brilliantly, Mal!" Ms Carmichael enthused as she patted Tybalt's shoulder.

Malory's fingers tightened on the reins. "OK."

There was an awkward pause until Dylan said pointedly, "We owe it all to you, Ms Carmichael. Thanks for all the extra coaching you've given us." She looked at Malory and raised her eyebrows pointedly, waiting for her to thank their instructor.

Tybalt snorted and pawed at the ground. "I'd better go cool Tybalt off," Malory said. "I don't want him to catch a chill."

As she rode away, she caught an expression of hurt flit over Ali Carmichael's face before she turned to congratulate Lynsey for the way she had ridden Quest. "You both put in a fantastic performance," she said. "Especially considering you had only a week to adjust to each other."

"Thanks," Lynsey responded. "And thanks for teaming me up with him. I admit it was a good choice."

138

It's like Lynsey and I have gone through a role reversal, Malory thought. *Usually she's the one being difficult and I'm the one going for damage limitation.* She sighed. It wasn't a role she liked, but right now she couldn't shake it off.

Malory took her time seeing to Tybalt after she had cooled him off. She wasn't in a hurry to bump into Dylan. Her friend had to be steaming after the way Malory had spoken to Ms Carmichael.

After she had strapped Tybalt's rugs on, she pressed her head against his smooth brown cheek. "I bet you can't work out why I'm not turning cartwheels. You try your heart out for me and all you get is me being miserable and bad-tempered." She drew her hand gently down his nose. "You deserve better than that."

"He's not the only one." Dylan spoke behind her.

Looking up, Malory saw her friend at the door. She tensed, waiting for the inevitable showdown, but instead Dylan said gently, "I know that you're finding things tough right now, but we're here for you. Even if we don't understand how you're feeling, it doesn't stop us from caring."

Malory's shoulders dropped a little. "I'm sorry. I guess I have been pushing you all away."

"And then some," Dylan agreed.

Malory crossed the stall. "I know I'm not acting exactly cool right now," she admitted. "But my emotions have gone into overdrive ever since I found out about my dad."

"You need to get together with him to sort this thing out," Dylan told her. "You can't keep going like this." She paused. "And I think Aunt Ali might well dunk you in the horse trough if you carry on cheeking her!"

Despite Dylan's teasing tone, Malory's cheeks burned. "My head tells me I owe them both an apology for the way I've been acting," she said. "But every time I think about going to sort it out, I feel all angry again about how they didn't involve me from the start."

Dylan sighed. "Well, just don't leave it too long before you sort it out. And when you decide to do something, I'll be right there for you."

Malory blinked hard. "You're the best," she said softly.

Dylan grinned. "No, *we're* the best," she corrected her. "And we have the trophy to prove it!"

11

After breakfast the next morning, Malory took an apple down to the yard for Tybalt. Hearing her footsteps, the polished brown gelding raised his head and let out a piercing whinny.

"Here." Malory held out the apple. "This is to say thank you for being so amazing."

Tybalt crunched contentedly on his treat for a few moments, then pricked his ears and gave another whinny, letting pieces of apple fall out of his mouth. Turning around, Malory saw her father standing a few feet away. He was waving a white handkerchief.

"I come in peace," he said. His tone was light but Malory noticed a nerve jumping in his cheek. "I just wanted to say that you were incredible yesterday," he added softly.

Ms Carmichael must have told him, Malory thought with a surge of irritation. It was starting to feel as if all the riding instructor ever did was interfere. *Couldn't she have let me tell him about the competition?*

"Tybalt was incredible," she said, turning back to stroke the gelding's velvety nose.

"You both were." Carl O'Neil came to stand beside her. "From the moment you took that first fence, I knew the trophy had your name written all over it."

Malory whirled around and stared at him. "You were here yesterday?"

Her dad smiled sheepishly. "I know you told me to stay away but when I spoke to Ali about it she convinced me that it wasn't really what you wanted."

"Why didn't you let me know you were here?" Malory gasped.

Carl O'Neil sighed. "I figured you might still be upset and I didn't want to do anything that was going to rock your concentration." He shrugged. "I didn't want to spoil your moment."

Malory felt her throat close. "The only thing spoiling my moment was thinking you weren't there," she said huskily.

There was a pause as Carl O'Neil reached out to stroke Tybalt. "I'm sorry. I really haven't handled things very well, have I?"

All Malory wanted to do was to throw her arms around her dad. Steeling herself to hold back, she said, "I think the worst thing was making me think you didn't want to date because you weren't over Mom."

Carl O'Neil paled. "I swear I had no idea that's what you thought." He reached out to grasp Malory's shoulders. "You know that I will never forget your mother, don't you?"

Daunted by the intensity in his eyes, Malory nodded.

"And nothing that happens to me now or in twenty years' time will diminish what we had." He swallowed. "But that doesn't stop me from getting lonely and, while the idea of going on an official date scares me, Al and I got chatting and somehow just fell into going out with each other." He hesitated. "You and I both know that no one is ever going to come along and replace your mom, but that doesn't mean I might not want to find someone who is special in their own way."

Malory suddenly felt very cold and very small. *I wanted to believe I was all Dad needed. How selfish am I? I'm surrounded by friends and getting on with my own life, but I'm expecting Dad to take what he can from the times we're together and go into comatose mode for the times we're not.* Bowing her head, she swallowed the lump that had bulged in her throat. *How could I have been so blind?*

She felt her father's arm slip around her shoulders. He held her close for a moment before saying, "Enough about me. How about you and this guy?" He patted Tybalt's neck. "Talk about an amazing partnership!"

Malory nodded. "Sometimes I feel like he can read my mind." She paused before forcing herself to look up at her dad. "I'm sorry." She didn't need to say anything else. Her father understood. Closing his arms around her he pulled her tight.

"I'm sorry, too. I should have told you what was going on right from the start."

Malory squeezed her eyes closed as tears rolled down her cheeks. "It's OK," she whispered.

"You're the most important person in my life." Carl O'Neil gently wiped her cheeks. "And Al understands that. It's the reason we've decided to have a break."

Malory pulled back. "What?"

"Maybe in time we'll pick things up again, but right now the only thing that matters to me is you," her dad told her. "You're not ready for me to start dating again, and I don't want to even think about it until you are." He smiled. "And when I give it another shot, I promise I'll do the whole thing properly and make sure you know exactly what's going on."

Malory couldn't stop the rush of relief at the thought of everything going back to normal. Then she paused, and listened to the little voice whispering inside her: Surely this couldn't be what her dad wanted? "I don't want you to stop dating Ms Carmichael because you're worried about how I'm feeling," she blurted out. "Please, Dad. Go and tell her that you've changed your mind."

Carl O'Neil shook his head. "The time's not right yet," he said. His eyes were warm but there was a hint of sadness in his voice.

Malory stared at him in dismay. She hated the thought of him throwing away his chance of happiness just because she had been selfish. "Please, Dad," she begged. She broke off as Tybalt reached over the door and nuzzled her dad's shoulder.

"Believe me, it's no sacrifice to concentrate on my lovely daughter," Mr O'Neil told her. "Family comes first, and I guess that includes you too, eh, boy?" He patted Tybalt. "Now." He turned to Malory. "How about since it's a Sunday, we go for a drive and stop off somewhere for a cream tea?"

"That sounds great," Malory said. She'd missed spending quality time with her dad. Today could be just about the two of them.

Because after today, I'm going to do everything I can to get Dad to change his mind. Operation Lunchdate was just a dry run. From now on, I'm going all out to get Dad back with Ms Carmichael!

"Wow, this looks really expensive," Malory commented as the car's tyres crunched over the gravel drive. Set back from the parking area was an imposing manor house with huge stone mullioned windows.

"I've got it covered," Mr O'Neil reassured her as he pulled up alongside a silver sports car. "Although I'm not saying I could bring us back tonight for a five course dinner!"

They walked up the steps and into the foyer where a smartly dressed receptionist led them to a lounge. "Someone will be along to see to you shortly," she smiled, handing them two dark green menus.

Malory sank back against the patterned cream sofa. "This is amazing," she said, admiring the fireplace which was big enough to stand in. A fire blazed in its hearth, filling the room with warmth. "How long ago do you think they used to live here?" She nodded at the portraits lining the far wall of people whose aquiline noses and strong chins marked them out as belonging to the same family.

"Actually, they still do." A tall, dark-haired waiter walked through the open door. "The De Lacys turned the house into a hotel two years ago but they still live in the west wing."

"It must have been quite a wrench, giving over so much of their home," Carl O'Neil commented.

"Yes, but without the hotel they would have sold up altogether," the waiter told them in an impeccable English accent. "And they greatly enjoy running it." He smiled. "Can I get you a drink?"

"We thought we'd try one of your cream teas," Mr O'Neil replied. "Although I suspect my daughter would like a hot chocolate." He raised his eyebrow at Malory.

"You got me," she agreed, thinking of the last time they'd gone out for a drink together. She'd been about to set him up with Matilda Harvey. *How naïve was I?* It felt as if months had passed since then, not just a few weeks.

They followed the waiter into the morning room which had sunlight streaming through French windows. Two other couples were sat at the tables with silver teapots and plates of tiny sandwiches set in front of them.

Mr O'Neil pulled out a chair for Malory to sit down before going to his own. Silver cutlery gleamed on top of the white linen cloth. Malory shook out her napkin and laid it neatly over her lap as if she did this sort of thing every day. After a few moments the waiter returned carrying their drinks and a china cake stand holding scones and a selection of cream cakes. He managed to squeeze everything on to their table and finished by setting down a side plate containing pots of clotted cream and strawberry jam.

"Will there be anything else?" he asked politely.

"No thanks, this is fine," Mr O'Neil replied. His eyes sparkled merrily at Malory as he offered her first choice of cakes.

Malory sighed with pleasure as she selected a giant chocolate éclair and sank her teeth into it. Light golden choux pastry gave way to an explosion of cream and chocolate. "Dylan would love it here," she said through a mouthful of sticky crumbs.

"She and Morello did well yesterday," Mr O'Neil remarked as he spread cream on a scone.

Malory felt a stab of guilt. "I never asked her how she did over the course!"

"She picked up two faults at the wall but apart from that it didn't look as if she and Morello put a hoof wrong," Mr O'Neil told her.

Malory felt proud of her friend. "She was dreading riding all of those turns. She must have been psyched she did so well."

"How come you didn't know how she'd done?" Carl O'Neil asked.

"Oh, it was pretty chaotic on the yard and I didn't get to see her for most of the day," Malory said. She didn't want to tell him that she suspected Dylan had been avoiding her. Picking up her napkin, she dabbed it on the end of her father's nose. "How did you manage to get cream there?"

"See how I need you around to look after me?" Mr O'Neil joked. "You have no idea the hardship involved in you staying away at school during term!"

Malory was distracted by the sound of metal pinging against crystal. She turned in her seat to see the husband of one of the couples standing up. Beside him, the waiter was holding a silver tray with six champagne flutes while a green glass bottle stood on a bed of ice in a silver bucket.

"I'm sorry for interrupting you," he said, smiling at Malory and Carl O'Neil and the young couple. "But my wife and I wondered if you'd raise a glass with us. We're celebrating our fortieth wedding anniversary today."

Malory clapped her hands along with the others, and when the champagne bottle was brought to her table the waiter handed her a ready-filled tumbler and murmured, "I hope lemonade's OK?"

"It's great," Malory said, raising her glass for the toast.

"I hope we'll be as happy in forty years' time as you clearly are," the young man called out as he raised his glass.

"We got married here yesterday," the pretty brunette alongside him added shyly.

As Malory shouted out her congratulations with the others, she glanced at her father. Although he was smiling broadly as he toasted the couples, Malory suspected he was painfully aware of being alone when so many people had someone special in their lives. *He doesn't deserve to be lonely*, she thought. *All he ever does is look out for me. It's about time I looked out for him, too.*

Malory waved goodbye to her father before hurrying to the Adams common room. She had agreed to meet up with the others for the first official meeting of the Crafty Club.

The table in the corner of the room was littered with raffia, scissors, measuring tapes, sheets of coloured paper and templates. A spool of ribbon was uncurling like a thin red snake, and a plastic tub of crystals stood perilously close to the edge of the table. Malory nudged it back towards the middle before the crystals spilled everywhere.

"Hey, Mal!" Lani looked up. "We've just started working on the design you found." She held up a piece of folded card with a design sketched out in pencil. "I thought I'd glue the ribbon in the shape of a baseball and bat," she explained.

Dylan rolled her eyes. "Yes, because baseball is the last word in romance this year."

"Something tells me Sam wouldn't go for the hearts and flowers look," Lani defended herself. She glanced at Honey. "Not that your card isn't gorgeous, of course."

Honey grinned as she used tweezers to add another crystal to her design of intertwined hearts. "Don't worry, I'm going to warn Josh to open it on his own!" She sat back, giving the tiny dab of glue a chance to dry. "How did it go with your dad, Malory?" she asked.

Malory sat on the chair alongside Lani. "Really good,

thanks. It was just so good to have things back on track."
She paused. "And that goes for you guys, too. I've been
such a pain lately."

Honey reached across to squeeze her hand. "It's OK.
You were going through a tough time."

Malory hesitated. "I don't know how I'm going to
make it up to Ms Carmichael. I've been so off with her."

"She's going to understand you weren't being
yourself," Honey told her.

Dylan nodded. "She'll know how bad you were
feeling about your dad dating again." She looked
meaningfully at Malory; Ali had obviously told her
about the break-up over Malory's reaction.

Malory hesitated. "I won't blame you guys for
burying me under the raffia when I ask you this, but I
was wondering if you'd help me set my dad up with a
date."

Dylan's scissors clattered on to the table. "What,
again? Who with?"

"Your aunt!" Malory exclaimed, realizing that Dylan
had misunderstood. She must have thought Malory
was happy for her father to date anyone other than Ali
Carmichael. "Look, I know I didn't react well to finding
out Dad and Ali were together but I've got my head
around that now. I want them to be a couple, really!"

Lani frowned. "But why do you need our help for
that? They're already dating."

"They were," Malory said. "They agreed to have a
break and now I can't persuade my dad that he doesn't
have to worry about my feelings." She looked straight

at Dylan. "I made a really big mistake, and if I could go back and do things differently, I would. I . . . I'm sorry I was so selfish."

Dylan's expression softened. "It's OK. I mean, it's not really, my aunt's terrific, and I think it would be great if she could find someone to date, but I guess I don't know what it felt like to be in your shoes."

"I think your aunt's terrific, too," said Malory. "And that's why I want to sort this out for her. And for my dad. He really likes her, I'm sure of it."

"What a mess." Dylan groaned. "And I'm not talking about the tabletop. OK." She clapped her hands. "Operation Matchmake, here we go!"

"It can't be anything like Operation Lunchdate," Lani pointed out. "Or Mal's dad is going to know what we're up to."

Malory nodded. "We've got to come up with a way of getting the two of them together that will seem totally natural."

Dylan suddenly jumped up, her eyes bright with excitement. "I know exactly what we need to do!"

The next evening Malory and Dylan walked down to the parking area opposite the outdoor arena. "So your dad didn't think there was anything suspect in you asking him to bring your other coat?" Dylan asked.

Malory shook her head. "I told him I wanted it for when I meet Caleb in town on Saturday." She grinned. "He's bringing it today because he thinks I need the rest of the week to match up an outfit with it."

"Here he is!" Dylan said, pointing to headlights sweeping along the single track road. "I'm out of here!"

Malory watched her run over to the judges' box outside the arena and duck behind it. Moments later the car pulled into the parking lot and stopped under the lamp post where Malory was standing. Bright yellow light spilled down on Carl O'Neil as he got out of the car.

"Hi, hon," he said with a smile. Opening the back door of his car, he pulled out a cream puffa jacket with faux fur lining. "Please tell me this is the right one."

"Perfect," Malory said, taking it from him. "Thanks for driving out with it, Dad."

"No problem," he replied. He reached out to give her a hug. "I'm going to head straight back. I've got a casserole due to come out of the crock pot."

Malory linked arms with him. "You can't leave without saying hello to Tybalt. It was only yesterday you were welcoming him into the family!"

Carl O'Neil grinned. "Well, I wouldn't want to give him rejection issues so soon."

"Exactly," Malory agreed, tugging him down the path towards the barn at top speed. She looked for Dylan from the corner of her eye but couldn't catch a single glimpse of her friend.

The moment they arrived on the yard, Malory slowed the pace right down. She wanted to give Dylan as much time as possible to carry out their plan. Her dad gave her a curious look as she practically dragged her feet across the concrete, but he didn't say anything as they walked into the barn. At the sound of footsteps, horses looked curiously over their stall doors. Tybalt kicked his door as they drew near.

"Looks like he can't wait to say hi!" Malory laughed. She took a horse cookie out of her pocket and gave it to her dad. "Remember how to give it?"

Her father put the cookie on the palm of his flattened hand and offered it to Tybalt. Tybalt gave a contented sigh as he crunched up the treat.

"OK, now you've had your supper I'm going to go get mine." Carl O'Neil stroked Tybalt's nose.

There had been plenty of time for Dylan to do what she had to, Malory decided as she walked back to the car park with her father.

Mr O'Neil gave Malory a hug and kissed the top of her head. "Lovely to see you, even if it was for just a minute," he said. "I'll give you a call tomorrow." He tried the door handle, but the door remained shut. "That's weird. I thought I'd left the car open." He frowned and patted his jeans. "I don't have the keys with me. I'm sure I left them in the car." He cupped his hands around his face and peered through the driver's window. "But they're definitely not there, so I must have taken them out."

Malory put on an innocent expression as he tried the door handle again. "Check your coat pockets," she suggested.

Her dad shoved his hands into each pocket. "No," he said. "They're not there. I don't know what I've done with them."

"Well, it's going to be hard finding them in the

dark," Malory pointed out. "I'll come down first thing tomorrow and find them. They're not going to be far."

"I'm just surprised I didn't hear them fall," her dad said, looking puzzled. "OK, I guess I don't have a lot of choice. Give me a ring tomorrow as soon as you find them." He sighed. "Now all I have to do is work out how I'm going to get home."

"Hi, Mal, hi, Mr O'Neil." Right on cue, Dylan appeared from behind the judges' box. "Is everything OK?"

"Dad's lost his keys," Malory told her.

"Oh, that's too bad." Dylan did a great job of looking dismayed.

"I'll be able to find them in the morning when it's light, but we were just wondering how Dad's going to get home," Malory said, hoping her friend wasn't going to lay it on too thickly with the amateur dramatics.

Dylan pretended to think for a moment. "I know! I could go and ask my aunt to give you a lift home. And if you have a spare set of keys she could bring you back again so at least you'd be able to take your car away tonight."

Malory didn't dare look at her father to see if he was falling for their ruse. But before he could respond, Mr McNulty, one of the grounds maintenance staff, walked up to his jeep, which was parked next to Mr O'Neil's car. "Is everything all right?" he asked.

Malory swapped a desperate glance with Dylan. "Everything's fine, thanks," she said.

"I've lost my keys," Carl O'Neil explained. "We were just debating a plan of action."

"You live in Cheney Falls, right?" said Mr McNulty.

Mr O'Neil nodded.

"Well, I'm clocking off for the night. If you have a set of spare keys, I'd be happy to run you over there to pick them up." Mr McNulty opened up his car.

"It's OK, thanks. My aunt will do it." Dylan said. "It makes sense, since she lives on campus."

Mr McNulty shrugged. "Whatever. It's not a problem for me to do it, either."

"That would be really kind of you, if you're sure," Carl O'Neil said appreciatively. He opened the passenger door of the jeep and smiled at Malory. "Sorry this has been a bit chaotic, love. Don't stay out here getting cold. I'll call you tomorrow to see if you managed to find my keys."

Malory's heart plummeted. Ms Carmichael was meant to be taking him home! *We hadn't planned on anyone else coming along and making the offer.*

"Bye, Dad!" she called as he ducked inside the jeep. Mr McNulty started the engine and backed out of the space. Malory waited for the jeep to leave the parking lot before she turned to Dylan. "Help!"

"It didn't exactly go to plan, did it?" Dylan pulled a face as she pulled the keys out of her jacket pocket and tossed them into the air.

"Which means we've got to come up with a new one," Malory said determinedly. "Right away." *Before Ali meets someone else, and my dad gets too shy to make another move.*

"How's he doing?" Malory stood on tiptoes to look over Bluegrass' door.

Lynsey looked up from bandaging the roan's leg. "He's starting to put some weight on it."

"That's great news," Malory enthused. "I bet you can't wait to get back on him."

"Obviously." Lynsey sounded out each syllable. "There's no other horse here in his league."

"Well, for a horse not in Blue's league, Quest turned in one heck of a performance," Malory responded. Biting back the rest of her irritation at Lynsey, she headed up to Tybalt's stall to lead him out for their lesson.

When she rode into the arena, Malory realized that she was the first rider in the class to be ready. Ms Carmichael was pacing the distance between four fences. Glancing up, she smiled at Malory. "How's our best rider?"

Malory felt herself blush. "Feeling like I owe you an apology," she admitted.

Ali Carmichael waved her hand dismissively. "Competition nerves can get to the best of us."

Malory halted Tybalt. She felt overwhelmed at the way Ali Carmichael was minimizing her rude behaviour. *How could I not have seen how perfect she is for Dad?* She desperately wanted to tell Ms Carmichael how wrong she'd been, but couldn't find the words.

"And I also wanted to say well done for whatever it was you said to Lynsey before the competition to change her attitude," Ali Carmichael added. She brushed her hands on her jodhpurs. "It really helped her to focus on Quest instead of pining for Bluegrass."

Malory was surprised. "How did you know I'd said anything?"

"I can't think of anyone else who could have worked such a transformation!" Ali Carmichael winked. "Not that I'm shocked. I've always had faith in your abilities as team captain."

Malory's blush deepened. "Thanks."

Tybalt pawed the floor, kicking up sand. Malory took the hint and returned her attention to him. She asked him to trot, and was working him on a twenty-metre circle when the rest of the class rode in. Ms Carmichael's generous words rang in her ears, and Malory felt as if a weight had lifted from her shoulders.

There's just one more thing I've got to put right now and that's getting Dad and Ms Carmichael together again. How hard can that be?

Malory kicked off her shoes and tucked her feet up on Honey's bed. Dylan slipped the DVD into her laptop. "I thought this movie might give us some ideas," she said as the screen title came up.

"*How to Lose a Guy in Ten Days?* Um, Dyl, you do know we're trying to get them back together, right?" Lani scooped up a handful of chips from the bowl on her bedside table.

"Duh. I thought we could do the exact opposite to whatever Kate Hudson does." Dylan rolled her eyes. "From now on there are to be no negative vibes, OK? I need to be on top form."

"Like when you came up with the car key idea?" Lani said dryly.

"There was nothing wrong with that plan." Dylan was defensive. "How was I supposed to know that a knight in shining armour would show up?"

"A knight in a four wheel drive," Malory corrected her with a grin.

"Food!" Honey interrupted. She picked up a Hershey bar and waved it in the air. "That's what we need."

"You want more? Didn't you get enough to eat at dinner?" Lani looked pointedly at the bowls of snacks on their bedside tables and dressing table.

Honey shook her head. "Not for us. For Operation Matchmake. Just think, you guys. It's a well known fact that the best way to a man's heart is through his stomach!"

Dylan wrinkled her nose. "That's always sounded totally gross to me."

"And what could be more romantic than a candlelit dinner for two?" Honey persisted, ignoring her.

Malory shook her head. "It's a nice idea but I'm not going to try to get my dad back to that restaurant. He'd know exactly what we were planning."

"I don't think we should ditch the idea totally." Dylan was frowning while she gave more thought to Honey's suggestion. "OK, so getting them into town might be a non-starter, but that doesn't mean we can't get them together for a meal somewhere else."

"Keep going," Lani encouraged as she picked up a soda and snapped back the ring pull.

"Well, how about we sort out a meal for them on campus?" Dylan asked. "We could arrange it for this Friday, Valentine's Day!"

"I don't see the student canteen as a springboard to romance," Malory said doubtfully.

Dylan looked disappointed. "Has anyone else got a better idea?"

"The barn!" Lani clicked her fingers. "It's got lighting, it's warm, and it's somewhere we could get Ms Carmichael to turn up without getting suspicious."

Malory felt a bubble of excitement expanding inside her. "This could work!" She looked around her friends. "But how would we get the food to them without it getting cold?"

"We'll come up with something," Dylan reassured her. "Apart from food, what else do we need?"

Honey pulled open the top drawer in her bedside cabinet and took out a notebook and pencil. "Candles," she scribbled.

"A table and chairs," Lani added.

"Tablecloth, cutlery, glasses and plates," Malory put in. "I wonder if the student centre would loan us some?" She pushed her hands through her hair. "This is going to take some organizing."

"That's what friends are for," Dylan reminded her.

"Thanks, guys," Malory said warmly. "I couldn't do this without you."

"Dylan wouldn't want you to." Lani grinned. "She loves playing matchmaker. I'd make use of her quick before she starts charging."

Dylan threw a pillow at Lani, who caught it neatly and tossed it back. "She shoots! She scores!" she crowed as Dylan fell back on the bed.

Malory snatched up the pillow and looked around. "Come on, you guys! We need to keep planning. Nothing's got to be left to chance this time. We've only got four days to make sure everything's absolutely perfect!"

During recess the next morning Malory went to find Mrs Herson. She found her housemistress sitting on one of the sofas in the student centre foyer.

"Hi, Malory." Mrs Herson looked up from the novel she was reading. "Isn't it a gorgeous day?"

"It's perfect riding weather." Malory glanced at the sunlight flooding through the windows. "Do you think there's any chance that Mr Westrop would let me off Geography to go for a trail ride?"

"It's unlikely!" Mrs Herson closed her book and took a sip of her latte.

Malory sat on the opposite sofa. "Mrs Herson," she began. "Can I ask you for a favour?"

"I'm afraid not even I can fix a trail ride instead of Geography for you." Mrs Herson smiled.

"It's not that." Malory hesitated. "It's actually to do with my dad and Ms Carmichael." She scrutinized her housemistress's face for a reaction but Mrs Herson kept her features perfectly composed. "I don't know if you knew they've been dating," Malory pressed on, "but I didn't exactly take it well when I found out."

Mrs Herson nodded sympathetically. Setting down her coffee cup she said, "I'm sure it was a difficult adjustment to make."

"I didn't even try to adjust," Malory admitted. "I guess you'd say I threw my teddy out of the pram and now Dad and Ms Carmichael have stopped seeing each other."

Mrs Herson raised her eyebrows. "And are you feeling any happier?"

Malory shook her head. "I feel like such an idiot. I know my dad needs more than just me in his life, and I've messed everything up for him." She took a deep breath. "So we've come up with a plan to try to get Dad and Ms Carmichael together so they can sort things out, and we were hoping you'd help."

"I assume you're talking about yourself and the other three musketeers, Dylan, Honey and Lani." Mrs Herson's eyes twinkled. "You'd better tell me what it is before I commit. If Dylan's involved, it's in danger of being a totally madcap scheme."

"Not this time." Malory grinned. "We thought we'd

set up a table in the barn so they can have a Valentine's meal but we're not sure how to sort out the food."

"Well, that doesn't seem too zany," Mrs Herson said thoughtfully. "I guess if we served a cold starter and dessert, it would just be the main course to worry about cooking and serving. If I drove it down in my car, it shouldn't get too cold. How about I put some ideas down for a menu and give them to you this evening?" She paused and looked straight at Malory. "I presume the favour you were asking wasn't my opinion of what you should do, but a little help with the catering?"

Malory tried to look sheepish. "Well, it would be totally awesome if you could really do all that."

Mrs Herson nodded. "It's for a good cause."

Malory's spirits soared. "Thank you so much, Mrs Herson!" Seeing Dylan and Honey walk through the double doors from the canteen, she jumped up. "Hey! Mrs Herson said she's going to do the cooking for us!"

Mrs Herson picked up her book. "Come and collect the menus from me after prep."

Dylan joined Malory in the centre of the foyer and gave her a high five. "We just spoke to the catering manager and she's promised to organize a table and cutlery for us."

"We asked her to take it down at seven to make sure none of the yard staff are around," Honey added.

"I love it when a plan comes together!" Malory beamed at her friends. "So all we need now is for Lani to come back from the barn with measurements, and we can start work on the banner. I'll call my dad tonight and ask if we can go out somewhere together on Friday evening. One of you can be waiting for him when he arrives to tell him I'm down at the barn. There won't be anything for him to suspect in that. And then Operation Matchmake will have lift-off!"

Later that evening, Malory left the others cutting out giant hearts which they planned to tape to the stall doors, and painting a banner which was to be strung across the aisle. In the foyer, she buzzed the door to Mrs Herson's private apartment and waited for her housemistress to answer.

"Here you go." Mrs Herson opened the door and handed Malory two sheets of paper. "I've put together two different menus. Decide which one you think your dad and Ms Carmichael will like best and get it back to me by tomorrow."

"I really appreciate this," Malory said.

"I'm glad you've involved me. I think it's going to be great fun." Mrs Herson's eyes sparkled. "I know the barn's got some heating but I've arranged for two portable heaters to be taken down just in case it's really cold. And I thought maybe I could invite Ms Carmichael to dinner on Friday night to ensure she's dressed up and hasn't eaten anything beforehand. I'll arrange for a call to come through asking her to go and check one of the horses on the yard."

"Wow, you're really good at this subterfuge!" Malory said, feeling slightly surprised. Thanking her again, she turned and ran up the stairs two at a time. "Menus!" she cried as she opened the door to her room.

"Read them out." Dylan looked up from the heart she was cutting out.

"Watch the scissors, Dyl," Lani warned, shifting further away as Dylan's blades waved perilously close to her.

"Oops, sorry," Dylan apologized. "I got distracted by the thought of food."

"I vote right now that Dylan's not a server on the night," Honey teased. "We need to make sure the plates get to the table without any bitemarks in the food!"

Stifling a giggle, Malory read out the first menu. "Chilled pea and mint soup followed by salmon and sauté potatoes and finishing up with lemon cheesecake."

"Please let there be leftovers," Dylan said.

Malory looked at the second sheet. "For Menu B's starter there's a prawn cocktail followed by Chicken Cacciatore and rice, and for dessert there's chocolate truffle torte. Which one do you think your aunt would prefer?"

"I think she'd go for either but the chocolate torte would win the day so I'd say Menu B," Dylan told her.

"Dad's a chocoholic too," Malory said, "so Menu B sounds a good choice to me. Right." She placed the menus on her bedside table. "Wish me luck, I'm going to go call Dad now."

"Good luck," her friends called as she stepped out into the corridor.

Malory crossed her fingers. *Don't let me down, Dad,* she thought, before realizing that maybe she didn't need luck after all. *He always comes through for me,* she thought with a rush of emotion. *Now it's my turn to come through for him.*

Stepping back from the table, Malory felt an attack of nerves every bit as bad as the ones before a competition. She reached out and repositioned the wine glasses for the umpteenth time.

The horses watched her curiously over their stall doors. Malory groaned as Morello gave an experimental nibble of the red crêpe paper stuck to his door. She hoped none of the others would have the same idea. Glancing up, she double-checked that the *Happy Valentine's Day* banner was secured out of reach. She wouldn't put it past Morello to try and yank it down.

Honey walked into the barn carrying two glasses. "Here's the prawn cocktail," she announced, setting each dish carefully down. "Dylan and Lani are waiting for your dad to arrive. Dyl's going to bring him down, and Lani will give Hersie the signal to phone Ms Carmichael."

Malory adjusted the wine bottle in its cooler and then exclaimed, "Music!" Hurrying into the tack room, she brought out the CD player. They'd put fresh batteries in, and chosen a selection of Bach concertos that Malory knew her dad loved. Placing it on an upturned bucket, she pressed Play and classical music filled the barn in a low background melody.

Honey switched on the small cordless lamp they'd borrowed from Mrs Herson to place in the centre of the table. Looking up, she gave Malory a reassuring smile. "That's everything sorted. All you have to do now is enjoy it!"

Malory nodded. "I just hope neither of them is cross that I'm interfering." She smoothed her hands nervously over the black dress she'd chosen to serve in.

Before Honey could answer voices sounded outside the barn doors. Malory hurried around to the back of one chair as Honey went to stand next to the wine chiller.

The barn door opened and Dylan looked in, flashing them a wide grin before stepping sideways for Mr O'Neil.

"Mal?" He glanced at the table and then at her. "Is this for us? I thought we were going out."

"I thought I'd surprise you," Malory said pulling back his chair. "Happy Valentine's Day, Dad."

"What a great idea!" He smiled and handed her a single-stemmed red rose. "Happy Valentine's Day, sweetheart."

Taking the rose, Malory laid it across the plate setting where Ms Carmichael would be sitting. "You look great," she said, admiring her father's open-necked white shirt and smart black trousers.

"Malory? Honey? What's going on?" Ms Carmichael burst through the barn door and hurried up the aisle. "I've just had a call to say one of the horses was looking colicky." She glanced at Carl O'Neil and then at the table set for two. "Oh!" Her cheeks flushed. "I didn't know anything about this," she said.

"Me either," Malory's dad said ruefully. He walked

around to the opposite chair and pulled it back for her to sit in. "But I have a suspicion that you're my intended dining partner for this evening. So, Ms Carmichael, would you care to join me?" Looking nervous, he gave a bow.

Ali Carmichael hesitated and Malory's heart seemed to stop as she wondered if her instructor was going to refuse to stay. She swapped a worried glance with Honey, who was biting her bottom lip.

"Stop!" Dylan suddenly cried out. Racing up the aisle, she stopped outside Morello's door and tried to wrestle away the entire crêpe heart he'd yanked off the door. She tore most of it free but there were still scarlet strands poking out of Morello's mouth. Wiggling her fingers into the side of his gum where there were no teeth, Dylan managed to flip the sodden paper out. "Eeugh," she said, shaking her hand.

"I do hope you're going to wash before you serve us." Ali Carmichael laughed and sat down. She looked up at Mr O'Neil. "I guess we might as well make the most of being waited on hand and foot!"

"As long as Morello stays safely inside his stall." Carl O'Neil's eyes twinkled. "I don't have Dylan's wrestling skills, and I'm afraid I'd have to abandon my place to him."

"I draw the line at eating with Morello," Ali Carmichael responded with a broad smile. "Although you'd be surprised at the amount of times I've found him attempting to break into my kitchen, and on one very memorable occasion, actually found him hoovering up the leftovers off the counter!"

Malory swapped a delighted glance with Dylan and Honey as her father and Ms Carmichael began to chat easily. As soon as they finished their prawn cocktail the girls cleared their glasses and carried them into the tack room. Using her mobile phone, Dylan called Lani to tell her they were ready for the next course.

Five minutes later Lani walked into the tack room carrying two plates of chocolate torte. "I've just served them the chicken," she reported. "They barely noticed me, they're so busy talking to each other!" She put the plates down on a bench before turning to hug Malory. "Are you still OK with this?"

Malory nodded, realizing that she was more than OK. It was wonderful to see how happy her dad looked as he talked with Ali Carmichael. "Thanks, guys, for all your help," she told them. "I couldn't have done this without you."

"No worries," Dylan told her. She grinned. "Would you flip again if I point out that we still might end up being related in the future?"

"Let me get used to my dad dating before I get my head around wedding plans!" Malory warned with a mock-horrified expression.

"I'm going to take her out of here before she produces a ring and puts it into Ms Carmichael's dessert," Lani said, linking arms with Dylan.

"I think giving your dad and Ms Carmichael some space is a good idea," Honey agreed. "We can come back later to collect everything up."

"I'll follow on as soon as I've served dessert," Malory told them.

Watching her friends leave the room, she thought for the millionth time how lucky she was to have them. With her arms hugged around herself, she sat on the bench and listened to her father's low laugh. *Just because he's moving on, it doesn't mean he's leaving Mom behind*, she thought. *She'll have a place in his heart forever.*

After she'd given enough time for the main course to be finished, Malory carried the plates of torte into the barn.

"Chocolate, my favourite!" Carl O'Neil and Ali Carmichael exclaimed in unison before laughing at each other.

Malory set the plates down on the table and met her father's gaze. "Has everything been OK?" she asked.

Putting his arm around her waist, he hugged her close. "Everything's been brilliant."

Without releasing Malory, he reached out to cover Ali Carmichael's hand with his own.

The moment was broken by Tybalt's high-pitched whinny. "I think he's saying that chocolate's his favourite too," Malory said.

"I'd like to thank you for tonight, Mal. It's been really special." Ali Carmichael's eyes glowed with happiness.

Malory smiled, suddenly feeling shy. "I hope it's the start of something really special," she whispered. A warm glow spread through her.

Something special summed up so much in her life. Now it was her father and Ali Carmichael's turn for something special, too.

Look out for more books
in the *Chestnut Hill* series

Lauren Brooke

Chestnut Hill

A Chance to Shine

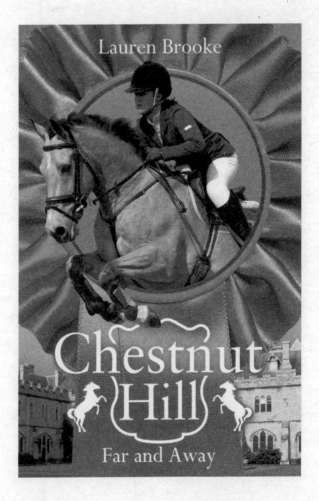

Lauren Brooke

Chestnut Hill

Far and Away